BOY RIDING

BEARYTALES
BOOK FIVE

SUE BROWN

Published by One Hat Press
First Edition
Cover design by Pippa Wood
Formatting by Format4U/Pippa Wood

ALL RIGHTS RESERVED

To my office pal, Clare London, for laughing at the right places in the story.

1

RED

They came in like avenging angels after Kingdom Water Theme Park closed for the evening. Men in various uniforms, others in black T-shirts, cargo pants, and more guns strapped to them than Red had ever seen, and hooded-eyed men dressed in dark suits and long coats, swarming in before anyone had a chance to run.

Red was rounded up along with the other boys and taken to the entrance to the park. He heard the words cops and Feds whispered between the boys. The first he knew, the second was a blank to him. He watched as the Green-coats, the men who had dictated his entire life, were arrested, and taken away in police vans.

Protesting loudly, the CEO who ran the theme park was forced into a van with no windows. As the doors on the van were slammed shut, the CEO, a man Red had only seen when there were issues, caught his eye. For some reason, the man's ice-cold and knowing gray gaze made a shiver run down his back.

"Don't worry about them, kid," a slender man said to him. He was maybe in his thirties, Red wasn't sure, but he had a weird accent. "They're going away for a long time."

Red turned to look at him. "What do you mean?"

"Cooper, you're needed." One of the cops waved at him.

The man raised his hand in response. "You've been rescued. Things can only get better now. Stay here." Then Cooper was gone, leaving Red staring after him.

A small group stood in the center of the chaos. They were an odd mixture of four men built like mountains, with bushy beards and deep blue eyes. It was clear they were related. With them were four younger, slender guys. It didn't take much to realize they were all couples, even the two standing further apart. He wondered if anyone else saw it or if it was only him.

Red noticed that everyone deferred to one of the smaller men. He was very young, with tousled, dark wavy hair, and an expression in his brown eyes as if he'd been to hell and back. Red recognized that expression. He'd seen it in all the boys in Kingdom over the years. All the men looked strained, but this one had the weight of the world on his shoulders.

A large guy with a stern expression, not a cop, maybe a Fed, approached the man. "We can't find any other boys, Lyle."

"How many did you find?" Lyle asked.

"One hundred." The large man grimaced and looked as if he were about to hurl. "We found their tower. It's behind the waterfall. There were three barely alive and one dead."

Red furrowed his brow. Why did that man call it a tower? The boys here called it the dungeon. Then Red processed what the man had said, and he bent over, unsure if he would puke. He dragged in deep breaths, trying to quell his churning stomach.

He wondered which one of the boys had died. Four of them had been dragged away yesterday for trying to flee. They were fools. He'd told them it was a bad idea. No one absconded from Kingdom in a group. On their own, maybe. There had been boys who'd escaped over the years and not been returned. But the rumors of what the Greencoats did to you when they caught you was enough to deter most boys.

Red had never tried to escape. What was the point? He had nowhere else to go. He'd never lived outside. That's what he called it. Outside. He had no idea what existed beyond the electric fences. He knew people lived different lives than him, because he watched all the visitors, the kids having fun with their moms and dads, and the groups of kids around their age screaming and laughing. None of them saw him.

"I wonder who died," he murmured.

"I heard it was Jamie," one of the boys standing next to him said. He was a few years younger than Red. "A Greencoat got him."

"Damn," Red muttered.

Jamie had been someone he looked up to. But he'd been warned about the punishment as they all had and chosen to ignore it. Now he'd paid the price.

"What's going to happen to us now?" The boy looked worried.

"Hell knows. Whatever it is, it won't be good."

Nothing was ever good for the boys of Kingdom Water Park, and whatever was happening now, wouldn't be any different.

———

Constance looked over her shoulder. "We're nearly at your new home, Red. Just try harder to settle, yeah?"

She was his social worker, but she'd reached her limit with Red. He'd heard her say it often enough. Now she was giving him to someone else. Three months of trying to deal with Red had driven her to the brink of the precipice. She'd collected him from the local sheriff's office, shoved him in a car, and told him there would be a long drive ahead.

Red didn't care. He would be gone as soon as they turned their backs. No one could keep him locked up now. This was what? Foster home number five? Although this time it was different. They'd taken him out of state. Constance had warned him to behave on the journey or the cop with them would handcuff him. He was a solid, silent presence at Red's side.

The car started to slowly climb the mountain road, the driver obviously not confident as he drove at a snail's pace.

"Where am I going?" Red rasped, his stomach clenching at the narrow road and tight curves.

"See the lights?" Constance pointed through the windshield.

He peered out of the window and saw twinkling lights far up the mountain.

"That's where we're going," Constance said. "It's a Christmas tree farm."

"No!" Red barked, his fists clenched, his voice shaking as he took in how high they had to go up the narrow road. "Turn back, find me somewhere else. I'm not going there."

"There's nowhere to turn around until we get there, kid," the driver said laconically.

The road went on and on and on.

"You can't keep me locked up forever," Red snapped.

Constance huffed. "Red, it's a foster home, not a prison."

"On top of a mountain."

"Lyle and his...family are good people."

Red leaped on the hesitation. "Family. What does that mean?"

"The Brenner brothers run the Christmas tree farm. They've lived on Kingdom Mountain their whole lives." She saw Red's eyes widen. "Oh yeah, this is where your water park got its name from. There was a theme park at the top of this mountain. Anyway, Lyle lives with his partner."

"You're giving me to a gay couple?"

The driver snorted but he didn't say anything.

Constance shot the driver an annoyed look, took a deep breath, and said, "Yes."

The driver barked out a laugh. "One couple? Try seven, kid."

"Seven couples?" Red croaked.

Constance's scowl grew deeper. "Lyle and his family are good men. Without them, we'd never have known about what was happening in the Kingdom theme parks. They don't need any homophobic attitude from you, young man."

Homophobic? That was a laugh.

"It was my home," Red muttered.

"You'll find a better one," she insisted. "Give Lyle a chance. And be kind to him. They've been through a lot."

Red stared out of the window, his lips pressed together in a thin line. They had no idea. No idea at all. He didn't care the brothers were gay. So was he. But he had no intention of telling anyone. His silence was one of the things that had kept him alive and unmolested in the water park. He knew about the chosen and the disappeared.

It took another hour before they reached the twinkling lights wrapped around a pine tree.

"We're here," the driver said unnecessarily. "Connie, we're gonna have to dump and run. I don't want to drive down in the dark."

Red glowered at him. He wasn't a goddamned package. The driver had a point though. It would be getting dark in a couple of hours. There was no way Red could get back down the mountain road to the nearest town now. He was stuck for at least one night.

The car pulled up outside a large cabin, with a wraparound verandah. Red squinted at it. The building seemed to go on forever.

"How many kids do they have here?" he muttered.

Constance gave him the side-eye. "None. Just you. There are seven brothers, remember?"

As they got out of the car, a door opened, and three men jogged down the stoop. He recognized two of them from the raid on the water park. The smaller, dark-haired one had to be Lyle. He looked more relaxed than at the raid. The third one he didn't know. He had to be one of the Brenner brothers as he was the size of a barn, but he had bright red hair, almost as vivid as Red's.

The cop held Red's arm. "Stay here," he ordered.

Red scowled at him. "I ain't going anywhere."

The cop was unmoved.

Constance's relieved huff was loud. "Lyle, it's good to see you again. Thanks for taking him in."

Lyle's smile was somewhat strained. "You obviously needed help."

She turned and beckoned to Red. "Red, come here. This is your new foster family."

Red didn't move. The cop gave him an ungentle shove and he only just kept his balance.

Lyle smiled at him. "Red, I'm Lyle. This is my partner, Gruff, and my...brother-in-law is probably easier...Harry. Welcome to our home."

Red said nothing.

"Well, I'll leave you to it," Constance said. "We want to get down the mountain while it's still daylight."

"Do you want an escort?" Harry asked.

"We should be fine." She turned to Red. "Bye, Red. Just stay put, yeah?"

Red said nothing and she sighed. Then she was gone with the silent cop.

Cowards! Running away from him.

"Come meet the others, Red."

Lyle didn't touch him, but kind of herded him into a large kitchen with a table surrounded by huge men. A small dog was sacked out in front of the range. It didn't stir at Red's appearance.

"I don't expect you to remember everyone's name," Lyle said with a chuckle. "But Damien is the oldest and the head of the household." He pointed to a large, broad-shouldered man with gray in his bushy beard who Red had seen at the raid. "You do what he says. The man mountain is PJ. He's the biggest and the middle one. You can ignore him." Lyle grinned at PJ's protest. "Gruff is the youngest and mine. If you feel ill, talk to Harry."

"That's me."

Red turned to see the flame-haired man standing behind him. Harry had the big bear look all the Brenners had.

"I also take care of the horses. You can find me in the stables."

Red nodded, although it was irrelevant to him. He would be gone as soon as they relaxed, and no one would find him again.

"We'll show you your room after dinner," Lyle assured him. "Sit here."

He sat Red in an empty seat and Harry sat next to him.

"I'm Matt," the young man said on the other side. He was vaguely familiar.

"I saw you at the water park," Red said, and Matt gave a curt nod.

Red looked at the large plate of shepherd's pie Lyle put in front of him with some dismay.

"It's okay," Lyle said soothingly. "Just eat what you can. Vinny and I are still getting used to three meals a day."

Lyle was right. The food was great. But he was used to one bowl of oatmeal a day. Red ate maybe a quarter, and he was full.

But Lyle just took it away without a word. "If you get hungry, you can ask me for food or help yourself to anything in the fridge."

"I'm not staying," Red declared.

"You have to stay for a while," Gruff said.

"I'm not staying, and you can't make me."

Suddenly all this...this... whatever was too much. Red bolted from the kitchen and stood at the bottom of the stairs, not sure where to go next. The rich food churned uneasily in his stomach. He had to get out of here. He had to.

HARRY

"We've got a bolter," PJ said cheerfully as he ladled hot chocolate into huge cups and passed them around the table.

"What gave it away?" Harry didn't bother to hide his sarcasm.

"I'll go talk to him," Lyle said with a sigh. He was curled up on Gruff's lap and didn't seem as if he wanted to move. "But I don't want to spook him."

"You stay here," Gruff ordered, wrapping his arms around Lyle. "Give him time to calm down and take a breath. He's spooked but he'll come back when he's ready."

"I thought Vinny was bad," PJ waxed on, "but this one's gonna be a menace if he's an escape artist. We can't hold onto him if he doesn't want to stay."

"I wanted to stay here," Vinny pointed out, poking his tongue out at PJ who just grinned. Since his return to the cabin, he and PJ had an easier relationship. PJ had eased up on the teasing, seeing the state all of them had returned in. PJ was like a gentle big brother to Vinny now...with the occasional teasing. "It was my big, bad Daddy who kept trying to push me out." He leaned into Damien who held him against his massive chest.

"I was trying to do the best for you," Damien grumbled. "And making us both miserable."

Vinny kissed his cheek. "Don't do it again."

Harry, the unofficial medic to the family, studied his brothers and their boys. He'd been worried about their mental health as well as their physical. The separation had been hard on them all and now they were back, they needed time to relax together, even Alex and Matt. The last thing they needed was additional stress from a stroppy kid who didn't want to be here.

He returned his attention to their unwanted guest. "What are we gonna do with him? We can't be watching him 24/7."

"What's his problem anyway?" Alec added. "You'd think he'd be pleased to be out of there."

"It's all he's ever known," Matt said quietly.

Alec studied him and gathered him in for a hug. Matt resisted for a moment, then leaned against him.

"We ripped his world from underneath him," Lyle agreed. "I don't think he can function in the outside world because the water park is all he knows. It was hard for him, but he was institutionalized. It's like being in a cult. If he's to survive, we need to deprogram him."

Gruff grunted. "That's not down to us, boy. We're just a family of gay Daddy bears, not specialists in handling traumatized men." Then he noticed the looks he was getting from the five boys sitting around the table. "What?"

Jack, PJ's boy, and the newest member of the Brenner family, rolled his eyes. "Three Kingdom boys and two boys abused by their family. Explain to me again how you don't know how to handle traumatized boys?"

"Don't be rude to Gruff," PJ admonished, then added, "Even if you are right." He kissed the top of Jack's head.

Harry intervened before Gruff could. "Gruff has a point. We're seven brothers who nearly fell apart after a few weeks of separation. It's one thing taking care of your boys, but another looking after a kid who doesn't want to be here. He should be in a foster home."

"The foster homes are overwhelmed since all the theme parks were closed," Lyle said. "If Red bolts again, the chances are no one will look for him. Constance, she's from

Child Protective Services, begged for our help. She's convinced he won't survive in the real world, no matter what he thinks. Even in the theme park, he was protected to a certain extent. He wasn't abused like Vinny. Red has no idea what it's like out there. How many wolves want to gobble up innocent boys like him."

"Then put him in a home," PJ suggested.

Lyle scowled at him. "No. He's going to stay here until the right foster home turns up or we find out he's eighteen. In which case we can't hold onto him."

"We're searching all the records we can find," Alec said, "but the water park kept worse archives than the mountain park. Jake and I are traveling back down to Florida tomorrow to see what we can find."

"Are you staying long?" Harry asked. "You know there's a storm due."

Alec leaned forward and patted his hand. "We'll be back by Friday. Aaron and Matt are coming with us."

"I haven't agreed—" Matt started.

"You're coming with me," Alec insisted, ignoring Matt's huff.

"I'll be fired."

"Then leave the job and work for us," Alec snapped. "How many times do I have to tell you?"

Matt subsided, refusing to meet Alec's furious eyes.

Harry took a deep breath, noticing the worried looks on his brothers' faces. Alec and Jake were local private investigators until Gruff brought Lyle home. Now they were deep in unraveling the Kingdom cult. It never used to bother the family if the two of them spent nights away from the farm. Their time apart had changed that.

Jake leaned forward and patted his hand. "It's okay, Harry. We've got return flights on Friday."

"I insisted," his boy, Aaron, said. "I don't like being away from the mountain."

"I think we all need therapists," Harry muttered.

Brad, who'd said nothing so far, just shrugged. "That's why I blow shit up. It's very therapeutic."

"Perhaps Red could help you," Lyle suggested.

Brad shook his head. "He's like a powder keg ready to go off. I'm not letting him near anything actually explosive. He should help Harry with the horses. They'll calm him down."

"He could peel potatoes," Vinny said.

Harry frowned. "No, I don't think so. I like coming to talk to you."

There was a chorus of "Me too," from the brothers. Vinny went bright red and buried his face in Damien's sweater. He hated peeling potatoes, but in a way, Vinny *was* like a therapist, the brothers joining him to talk about their frustrations of the day.

"Horses it is," Lyle said.

Harry stared at him, horrified. "He might be afraid of them."

"He's got to do something," Lyle said, "and you need help."

"I was gonna ask Matt," Harry pointed out. "At least he knows how to take care of our animals."

Matt gave a wry chuckle. "I've got a job that takes up all my time. I don't need another one. No matter what Alec says."

It was on the tip of Harry's tongue to make a crack about Alec and Matt finally working it out, but the misery on their faces was enough to make him hold back.

Then he had another thought. "We could lock the doors

overnight, but Red will find a way to get out if he's desperate enough."

"He's not going to make it down the mountain road in the dark," PJ said. "It will take him hours to walk down to town."

Gruff snorted. "Just remember not to leave your keys in the trucks."

"Like any of us would do that." Harry sprung to his feet at the roar of an engine. "Oh fuck. That's mine."

"You fucking idiot," PJ yelled. "Come with me. We'll follow him."

"Dollar from both of you," Damien barked. "Go get him back. Don't scare him off the side of the mountain."

Throwing a dollar on the table for the swear jar, Harry bolted to the door, shoved his feet in his boots, and grabbed his coat. PJ was beside him, and they ran for PJ's truck.

"Do we even want him back?" PJ muttered as he started the engine.

"He's a kid who needs help," Harry said. "He may be a pain in the ass, but I wouldn't want anyone running away from us in the dark and putting himself in danger...and I want my truck back in one piece."

PJ shot him a quick look. "I guess you're right. But I hope he's got the sense to go slowly down the road."

"Keep well back. If nothing else, let's get him to the town and then we can put him on the first bus outta there and get my truck back."

Except they discovered Harry's old Chevy by the twinkling lights, the engine still running, but not moving.

PJ pulled up behind him and cut the engine. "Go on then. Find out what's wrong."

"Why me?"

"It's your truck. Get on with it."

Harry huffed at the order and jumped out of the truck, approaching cautiously in case Red decided to speed away.

He opened the driver's door to see Red staring straight ahead, hands curled into fists around the wheel. He didn't blink or turn to look at Harry.

"Red?" he asked gently. "Are you all right, kid?"

"It's so high." Red's voice was so thin, it was eerie.

"What is?"

"Here. I can't see anything. I could drive off the road and fall forever. I've never..."

Harry understood. At least, he thought he did. Red was shit scared. He reached in and took away the keys, slipping them into his pocket. "Let's go home. Okay?"

"It's not my home."

"I know," Harry soothed. "But at least tonight, you can sleep somewhere safe and warm. We can talk about it in the morning."

"I don't want to be here," Red insisted. "I want to go back to my home."

That wasn't a conversation Harry was going to have now.

"Just come back for tonight." Harry gently eased Red out of the truck and reached in to pick up his pack. The boy followed as if his brain had taken a sudden vacation and his body was just following Harry's orders.

That was fine with Harry. He gave the truck's keys to PJ and walked Red back to the cabin.

Red balked on the stoop. "I can't—"

"You're not the first to run," Harry assured him. "Just come inside."

The kitchen was empty, but Harry just led Red up the stairs to the small bedroom. Matt usually slept there but he'd agreed to share with Alec while Red needed the space.

Red stood in the middle of the room while Harry dumped his pack on the small bed.

Harry took Red's shoulders. "It's too dangerous for you to leave tonight. Go to sleep and we'll talk in the morning."

Red nodded and sat on the bed.

Harry patted his shoulder and left the room to find Gruff and Lyle waiting for him.

"Do we need to lock the doors?" Lyle asked quietly.

Harry shrugged. "He's agreed to stay the night. After that, who knows?"

2

RED

Everything was wrong. Red was too warm, the bed was too soft. Where was the noise of boys talking and bickering with each other? Where was Chuck booming at everyone to be ready before the Greencoat turned up to inspect them?

Red had processed all this before he was fully awake. Where was he? He opened his eyes, sat bolt upright, and looked around, panicked by the small room. It had a bed that took up most of the space, a tiny dresser, and three shelves holding children's books. That was it.

He didn't know this room and he could feel the walls closing in on him. He had no idea where he was. He had to get out of here, but he just knew the door would be locked. What had he done? Why was he locked in?

"Oh great, you're awake."

Amid his panic, Red completely missed the door opening.

"Red?"

Red blinked and focused on a slender man staring at him, his brows furrowed. Who was he? Red had seen him before. Maybe at the water park. Why was he here? The park wasn't open to customers yet. Red tried to tell him this, but no words would come out. It was as if he'd forgotten how to speak. He clutched at his throat.

"Red, are you all right?"

The man stepped closer to him, but Red backed away, fighting with the bedclothes until his back was pressed against the wall and he had nowhere to go. He couldn't breathe, couldn't force the air into his lungs. Black spots prickled at the edges of his vision and the only sense that seemed to be working was his hearing.

"Okay, Red, you stay there a moment. Harry, I need you."

Red wasn't going anywhere. Not until his mind quit racing around and he worked out who these people were and where he was and what he was doing here.

Then another man appeared. Huge. Bushy beard. He had red hair just like him. Red knew he'd seen him before, but his mind was racing so fast he couldn't focus.

"I'm here. What can I do?"

"Red's having a panic attack."

Harry nodded and came into the room. That was worse. He was so big, he seemed to swallow up all the oxygen in the room. Red couldn't get away from him.

"No. No." Red stared at him, wide-eyed.

"Red, you're safe. I'm not gonna hurt you." Harry moved closer and sat on the bed. "I just need you to breathe, okay?"

Breathe? I'm breathing. Of course I am.

"Open your eyes. Look at me."

My eyes are closed?

Red opened his eyes and stared into deep blue pools. Harry didn't touch him, but Red couldn't focus on anything else.

"Well done, boy. You have gorgeous blue eyes. Now, breathe in. And out. In. And out."

Red focused on Harry's rumbling voice and a little of the panic receded.

"In. And out. Just follow my breathing."

I can do that.

Red did nothing but breathe in time with Harry until he was breathing normally again. It seemed an eternity, but then Harry smiled at him.

"Good boy, that's it. You're back with us again."

Red licked his lips, his mouth suddenly dry.

"Do you need a drink?" Harry asked. At Red's nod, he called out, "Lyle, please could you fetch a glass of water for Red?"

Lyle. That was his name. I remember. Constance brought me here. The mountain! I should have gone by now!

Red's heart started pounding again, his hands were clammy, and his vision blurring.

"Slow your breathing, Red. It's okay. I'm here and you're safe."

Harry held a glass of water to Red's lips. Red choked a little and tried to hold the glass, but Harry said, "Let me. Your hands are shaking."

Red put them in his lap. He hadn't even noticed. He took a few swallows of the cool liquid, feeling it slide down his throat, and it eased the tightness enough to make it easier to breathe. He whimpered as Harry took the glass away.

"Lyle will fill the glass again," Harry said, and Lyle disappeared with it.

They sat in silence, which Red appreciated. He wasn't ready to talk yet.

Then Lyle returned and this time Harry gave the glass to Red. His hands still shook, but he managed to drink without spilling too much. Again, Harry sat patiently. Lyle had vanished, leaving him with the big man.

"I feel better now," Red muttered.

Harry said nothing. He seemed to be waiting for something. Red racked his brain to think what it could be. Then he guessed.

"Thanks."

"Good boy. Are you ready for breakfast now?"

"We don't eat breakfast," Red said, confused why he felt so pleased by the unexpected praise.

"We do here. This is not like the water park. You get three meals a day and all the snacks you want."

"I'm not hungry."

Red wanted Harry to leave him alone so he could sneak out. But Harry stood and looked down at him.

"Come downstairs. I know this is hard for you, but you need something, even if it's just a cup of hot chocolate. We've been through this before."

Harry wasn't going to go without him, Red knew that. He didn't want to be punished. Harry wasn't a Greencoat, but that made him unpredictable. Red didn't know what to expect. He wanted his old life back. He understood it.

Red had slept in his clothes, so he just got up and followed Harry down the huge carved staircase, stopping halfway down as he looked at a small framed picture. He leaned in to check he wasn't seeing things.

Harry turned, obviously realizing Red had stopped. "Yes, it's a pack of coffee beans. Well, elephant poop."

"Elephant poop?" Red said, not believing his ears.

"Don't worry, I'll explain another time," Harry said, chuckling. "It's all about Jack. But no one's gonna drink elephant poop coffee so he stuck it on the wall."

Red shook his head and followed Harry into the kitchen. Unlike the previous night, it was empty apart from Lyle and Vinny who sat at the table with books in front of them. A black dog with a white heart on its chest rushed over to sniff him. Harry scritched the dog behind its ears and it closed its brown eyes in ecstasy.

"That's Rexy. He's mine," Vinny said.

Red wasn't sure about Vinny. He seemed kind of fierce. But the dog was cute. One of the Greencoats had a dog and sometimes Red walked it. It was old though and not as bouncy as Rexy.

"Red needs some hot chocolate and then he'll see if he can eat," Harry said.

Lyle nodded and Vinny gave him a sympathetic smile.

"You'll soon get used to eating again. There's always food here." Lyle went to the stovetop and ladled something from a pan into a cup. It smelled very sweet. "Vinny and me still struggle at times."

"I'm not staying," Red said.

Then Harry eased him into a seat. "Just sit down." He took the cup from Lyle and handed it to Red. "Drink up. Doctor's orders."

Red stared at him. "You're a doctor?"

Harry rumbled out a laugh. "Not even close. I just do what needs to be done. I'm off to the stables. I'll leave you boys to talk. Drink."

He left the kitchen with that order. Red stared after him, feeling like he was losing his only ally.

Obediently, Red took a swallow of the hot chocolate before he realized what he was doing. It was thick and sweet and had a kick. He wasn't sure he liked the taste, but he sipped at it, not wanting to offend Lyle.

He expected Lyle and Vinny to start questioning him, but they went back to reading their books. Red drank his hot chocolate until he noticed he'd finished the whole cup.

"Would you like more?" Lyle asked, his expression kind.

Red wasn't sure. His stomach churned a bit. "No… thanks. I think I need to wait."

Lyle nodded understandingly. He went back to his book.

"What are you reading?" Red asked, thinking he ought to say something.

Lyle turned the book in front of him so Red could see it. It had pictures of animals on the pages and not much writing. "Vinny and I weren't taught to read or write, so Gruff is teaching us. We haven't had much time to practice."

Red caught Vinny's almost hostile stare. "I can do math because I worked in the offices but I'm not good at reading or writing," he confessed, seeing Vinny's expression ease a fraction. "The Greencoats taught me what I needed to do the job."

"Didn't your foster family—families—take you to school?" Lyle asked, his brows furrowed. "They were supposed to."

"I ran away before any of them could." Red scowled. "I'm too old to go to school with small kids."

"Were they mean to you?" Vinny asked.

Red had to think about that. "I don't know. I don't think so. I didn't understand what they wanted me to do. I've only ever lived in the water park."

Vinny nodded. "I don't remember anything else. My father gave me to Kingdom Mountain because he couldn't look after me."

"I had parents but they were killed when I was six," Lyle said. "Vinny and I grew up together."

"How did you end up here?" Red asked.

That wasn't what he wanted to ask. He wanted to know why the two men, boys really, had decided to turn his world upside down. He'd been happy. As much as you could be in the water park. He kept his head down and did the work and never ended up in the dungeon.

He wanted to yell at Lyle and Vinny and tell them how much he hated them for destroying his life. Instead, he listened to Lyle's story of the worst and best day of his life. The day he was disappeared.

HARRY

Harry felt a bit of a coward for running away and leaving Red with Lyle, but he knew his family. If he showed any sign of interest in Red or spent too much time with him, his brothers would assume they would become a couple, and he claimed Red as his boy.

Harry didn't want a boy. The past few months had convinced him of that more than ever. Yeah, he sometimes envied his brothers' contentment with their boys and the chance to train them, but Lyle's arrival had turned the Brenners' easy existence upside down and Harry wasn't sure he could get over that.

He'd liked his life of tending the horses, the occasional medical issue, and nights down at the Tin Bar. Now even his longtime drinking partner, PJ, was otherwise engaged with his boy. Where did that leave Harry? Alec and Matt were together, even if Matt wouldn't admit it, and Brad just wanted to blow things up and write poetry about it. Brad was like Harry, content with his own company.

Harry needed a night in town, away from them all. And then he felt guilty because he'd been as thrilled to see his brothers return from their trip as any of them.

He spent a long time fussing over Damien's horse, Thunder. The black stallion was bad-tempered with most people. Just like his owner. Although he was as much Harry's as Damien's now, considering how little time his brother spent with Thunder. The grumpiness still applied. Thunder liked Harry, probably for the treats that were always in his pocket and the care that Harry took. Harry looked at the row of seven horses. He had a feeling they wouldn't be replaced. Only Damien, PJ, and Gruff worked on the farm, and both Damien and Gruff spent most of their time dealing with the Kingdom issue. Jake's boy, Aaron, had talked about helping but Harry hadn't seen him beyond mealtimes.

Would they end up selling the farm? Harry shuddered at the thought. But the family wasn't wealthy, and this was draining their resources.

He leaned against Thunder's strong neck. "What are we gonna do, Thunder?"

Maybe he could go train to be a vet like he'd always wanted. His brothers didn't need him now.

"Would you like that?" he murmured into Thunder's neck. "I'd know what I was doing instead of the half-assed approach you get now." At Thunder's reproachful stare, Harry sighed. "I do my best."

"Feeling insecure?"

Harry turned to see Brad in the barn doorway. "How much of that did you hear?"

"Not much. What's up, little brother? You look like you're having a crisis."

Harry wasn't surprised to find Brad here. As well as

writing poetry and being able to deliver a damn good haircut, Brad always seemed to know when his brothers needed a shoulder.

Brad and Damien both took after their father. Strong faces, thick brown hair, and a bushy beard, although Damien had been convinced he was ugly until Vinny showed him otherwise. Harry had always wished he'd ended up with brown or chestnut hair. He looked just like his brothers but with fiery red hair from an uncle on his dad's side, way back. His mom had named him after a prince in England somewhere. Harry just smiled when people made a crack about it. Red hair and freckles didn't stop him from getting attention from the boys. They always stopped to talk about his hair and wonder if his body hair matched. It did. He idly wondered if Red had the same issue. Did he have any body hair at all?

"Harry?"

"Sorry," Harry said, knowing he was blushing. "I'm just...do you think we still need seven horses?"

Brad frowned. "You think we should get rid of them?"

"Most of you don't ride anymore. Even Gruff is always on the road with Lyle."

"But that's short-term, Harry. When it's all over, Gruff will be back working the farm."

"Maybe."

Brad raised an eyebrow. "You don't think so?"

Harry huffed. "I think Gruff is following his true calling."

"Protecting Lyle?"

"Teaching. You know he's always wanted to teach. Now he has the chance."

Brad's expression changed. He knew, like all the brothers, Gruff had always wanted to become a teacher. None of them had followed their dreams, the money hadn't been there.

"What about your burning ambition, little brother? Do you want to become a vet?"

"Maybe I'm too old." A tacit admission Harry had been thinking about it.

"You're not too old. If we sell the horses, you'd be free to focus on your studies."

Brad didn't seem fazed by his brother's sudden admission, which was a relief to Harry.

"I've been studying online," Harry admitted. "I didn't want to leave while...I just didn't want to leave."

Brad nodded. "We needed you here. But it won't be forever."

"What about the farm? PJ can't work it alone."

"I'm here, and there's Jack and Aaron. Vinny offered to help. Anything to get away from the potatoes. They'll learn fast enough. We all had to."

"They're little guys," Harry protested.

"Harry," Brad said gently, "you're just finding excuses not to go."

Harry pressed his lips together. "If I do study, I won't go out of state. I won't go too far."

To his surprise, Brad loped over and gave him a fierce hug.

"You do what you need to do to make you happy."

Even though they were of similar height and build, Brad was reassuringly solid to lean against.

Harry raised his head to look at him. "And you? What makes you happy?"

Brad gave him a wolfish grin. "Blowing shit up and writing about it. I'm a man of simple pleasures."

Harry returned his grin with a flat stare. "Dude, I've

read your poetry. There's nothing simple about it. I don't know what half the words mean."

"I could explain."

"Don't. Just don't," Harry begged. "I understand animals, not words."

Brad snorted. "You're safe. But you're forgetting one thing."

Harry stared at him, uncomprehending. "What?"

"What about Red?"

"What about him?"

"If he's your boy, he needs you. Will he go with you to vet school?"

Harry glared at him. Seriously. Already with this? "He's not my boy."

"Uh-huh."

"Don't start," Harry snapped. "Anyway, he's just got here and he's desperate to leave. He doesn't want a Daddy and I don't want a boy."

"We don't always get what we want," Brad rumbled.

"He could be straight or vanilla," Harry pointed out. "Not every lost boy is one of us."

Brad smiled, squeezed Harry on the shoulder, and left the barn.

"What's that supposed to mean?" Harry yelled after him, then apologized to Thunder who shifted restlessly. "Sorry, boy. He drives me nuts, you know? All cryptic and shit. Why doesn't he just say what he means?"

Thunder just gave him a snort, but the answer was obvious. Because he was Brad, and he was a poet, and he was always cryptic and shit.

Going away to vet school. Huh. He'd expected Brad to be against it. They hadn't coped when Alec, Jake, Gruff, and Damien went on their road trip. Damien and Vinny had given up on their solo road trip because they wanted to be here. Yet, Brad seemed laid back by the idea of Harry being away for months at a time, maybe forever.

"I don't know whether to be hurt by that or not," he admitted to the horse.

"Do you always talk to the horses?"

Harry turned to see Red staring at him. He was dressed in an old jacket with a beanie and gloves. shrugged. It wasn't the first time he'd been asked the question. "They like it. It settles them. What are you doing out here?"

"Lyle and Vinny told me to find you. They wanted to get rid of me." Red's mouth was twisted. "They were waiting to see if I'd run."

"Are you going to?" Harry asked bluntly.

"What are the chances of me getting down the road without one of you finding me?"

Harry gave a wry smile. "No chance at all. If you're on the road, we'll find you and there aren't many places you can hide."

"That's what I thought." Red didn't sound resigned to the idea. He sounded angry. Really, furiously angry.

"You don't have to stay here, kid. We can find you another family," Harry pointed out.

He knew Lyle had moved kids from Kingdom Mountain who weren't happy in their new foster homes. Like Red, not all of them found it easy to adjust to life outside the theme park.

"I don't want another home," Red yelled.

Thunder shifted and shook his head.

"Let's take this outside. The horses don't like yelling." Harry pet Thunder to calm him.

Red snorted and rolled his eyes, but he did stalk outside the barn, and he waited for Harry to join him, glowering at him, his hands shoved under his armpits trying to keep warm.

Harry shivered in the chill wind. The temperature had dropped several degrees since he'd been dealing with the horses. It had to be arctic for Red, coming from Florida.

"You don't wanna be making your escape now," he advised the boy. "There's a storm coming."

"How do you know?"

"Lived here all my life. You don't want to be caught on the road in the storm. It's easy to fall off the side of the mountain. You should go back in the cabin."

"Maybe that's what I want to do," Red muttered.

Harry squinted at him. "What do you mean?"

Red shrugged. "Fall off the side of the mountain. It's not like anyone cares if I live or die."

3

RED

He'd expected a look of horror from Harry. Protestations that of course, he cared. Instead, the man seemed indifferent. That stung. Red needed something to push against. How could he rebel against indifference?

"Does it matter what anyone else thinks?" Harry asked, shoving his hands down into his jacket pockets.

"What?" Red stared at him, confused.

"Do you care what I think about you?"

"No," Red snapped.

"Lyle? Vinny?"

"No!" Red said scornfully. "They think they're better than me."

"That's not true," Harry said. "They're...they were just like you. Kingdom Mountain was just the same."

Red refused to meet his gaze. "They've got a family now. They think..."

Harry held up a hand, his expression stern. "Let me stop

you there. If you're gonna be rude about my brothers or any of their boys, we're gonna fall out. Think very carefully about what you're gonna say next."

"You all judge me!"

"I think you're the one judging us," Harry said. "Lyle just wants to take care of you."

"He took away the only home I had." Red's voice cracked and he had to breathe deeply not to show Harry how upset he was.

"I know he did, and none of us are gonna apologize for that. You don't know how many boys he's saved from death, including you."

"You're lying!" Red burst out.

"I'm not." Harry looked up into the white, snow-filled clouds. "I hope Jake and Alec are safe. They're flying out today. I've got to make sure the horses and the chickens are ready for the storm. You can help me or go. I don't care. Remember what I said about walking down the mountain in the storm though? You should wait for better weather. It'll take hours to get down the road."

He did seem indifferent whether Red stayed or went. Red took a deep breath and nodded.

"I'll help. Tell me what to do."

"Good boy. Put extra hay in each stall except Thunder. I'll do him. He needs time to get to know you. The others are mares, they're all sweethearts. Be careful of Star. She's cheeky and likes to take a nibble if you're not paying attention. Check on the salt licks in each stall. Then we'll spread salt on the paths."

"What about water?"

Harry nodded approvingly. "The automatic water feeder was designed by Brad. It won't freeze."

Red didn't know much about horses, but these were

well-groomed and friendly, and the barn was well-main-
tained. The mares seemed pleased to meet a new face and
he made sure to give them all attention. Star did try to
nibble him, but he gave her a pat and a carrot Harry handed
him, and they made friends.

He left Thunder alone. The huge, black stallion was too
much horse for him.

By the time they'd finished, the snow had started to fall.
Harry pointed toward the chickens.

"Let's just check them over, pick up any eggs, give them
food, and shut them in for the storm."

"How long will it last?" Red asked, his teeth chattering,
as they hurried to the large enclosure. He was glad of the
gritted paths. His boots were old and worn, with little tread
left. He'd been waiting for replacements when they were
forced out of the park.

"A day, maybe two," Harry rumbled.

Red stared at him in dismay. "That long?"

He'd wanted to get on the road by the end of the day.
Surely someone would take him into town.

Harry stopped and looked at him. "Red, just take a deep
breath before you try to run away again, yeah?"

And that was it. He carried on walking, leaving Red
staring after him. Red gritted his teeth. He was leaving, no
matter what Harry said.

But twenty minutes later as they hurried to the cabin,
heads down against the roaring wind and snow, Red knew
he wasn't going anywhere. He could barely see beyond the
end of his nose. If it hadn't been for Harry's tight grip
around his bicep, he felt sure he'd have gotten lost and
never found the cabin. Harry shoved open the door and
they stumbled inside. The silence after the noise outside hit
Red like a brick wall. It was almost eerie.

"Take your jacket and boots off," Harry ordered. Then he frowned as he looked at Red's feet. "Your feet must be frozen. I'll find you new boots. You'll need them if you're gonna help me outside."

Red opened his mouth to say he didn't want anything from Harry when Lyle appeared from the kitchen, a look of relief on his face when he saw Red.

"Oh good. You're back. I wasn't sure if...well, I'm glad you're safe."

And that made Red annoyed at the guilt he felt for worrying Lyle. "I'm fine," he said shortly.

Harry gave him a sharp look, before asking Lyle, "Where's Brad?"

"He's on his way," Gruff said, appearing behind Lyle "He was going to ride it out in the barn, but Damien ordered him in. The storm is gonna be worse than they originally predicted. Will the horses be okay?"

"They'll be fine. They've got plenty of hay and water. The chickens are shut up too. Red helped me."

Gruff nodded, and Lyle beamed at Red as though he'd done something special. Red's stomach churned. He didn't want them to like him or be pleased with him.

"Come get hot chocolate before PJ drinks it all," Gruff said.

"Fuck off," PJ muttered.

"Dollar," they all chorused.

"It's a swear jar," Harry said to Red. "It pays for Thanksgiving. Well, PJ mainly pays for it."

From the grumbling Red could hear, PJ wasn't impressed.

Red gave a short nod. He'd never experienced Thanksgiving. Every day was like the last in the water park.

"Wait here," Harry said to Red and jogged up the stairs.

"Come in the kitchen when you're ready," Lyle said and let Gruff pull him back there.

Which left Red standing alone in the hall, just like he always was.

A minute later, Harry jogged down the stairs and handed Red a thick pair of socks.

"They're too small for me. Your socks are wet. Take them off."

Red sat on the bench without thinking, peeled off his sopping, thin socks with some difficulty, and tugged on the bright red pair Harry gave him. They were too big, but so warm and soft. Red had never had socks like them.

Harry gave an approving nod and guided him into the kitchen.

"And Aaron and Jake are staying at the motel until the storm is over. They were halfway to the airport when they heard their flights were canceled," PJ was saying to Damien. "They're almost there. Alec and Matt decided to visit the lead Cooper sent us instead. They won't be back until Friday."

Red noticed none of them seemed happy. He looked up at Harry to see the same expression.

Harry caught his glance. "You'll learn soon enough. We don't cope with being separated."

"Does Matt work for Alec and Jake?" Red asked.

Gruff snorted. "Who knows? They certainly don't."

"At least Alec is happier when he can take care of Matt," Damien said, and they all nodded.

Red wanted to scream at the brothers' contentment. They had no idea. No idea at all. Then he caught Vinny regarding him with a knowing expression. Red wasn't the only one in the room who'd lived through hell, he had to remember that.

"Sit down, guys." Lyle held out two large cups. "Drink this." He chewed on his bottom lip. "Do you think you should look for Brad, Da..." Then he shot a quick look at Red. "...Gruff?"

Da...? Whatever Lyle had intended to say, Red could see Gruff wasn't happy he'd changed it.

As Harry tugged Red over to the table, the kitchen door opened, and Brad stepped in. At least, Red thought it was Brad under the layer of snow.

PJ howled with laughter. "Hey, Santa Claus. You're too early for Christmas."

Brad rolled his eyes and wriggled like a dog shaking its wet coat. "It's got bad real quick out there. The boys aren't coming up the road, are they? I heard their flight was canceled."

"They're staying in town," Harry said. "Drink up, Red. You're shivering."

All eyes turned on Red and he blushed. He hadn't even realized.

"We'll finish this and go upstairs and find you a warm sweater," Harry said. He grinned at Red's skeptical expression. "We have trunks of clothes in the attic. We weren't always this huge and Mom never threw anything away. All the boys start with those."

Red grunted. He couldn't stay in the same clothes forever, but he wasn't a charity case. He excused himself to use the bathroom to get over his irritation.

On his return, Red stopped on the threshold as he heard Gruff's question.

"Why did you stop?"

Stop what?

"I don't know how much Red knows," Lyle admitted. "He could cause trouble for us."

Red frowned. What kind of trouble? He wanted to go back to his own home, and not cause trouble for the Brenner family.

"He lives in our house," PJ pointed out. "We can't hide it from him forever. And I'm not gonna walk on eggshells in my own home, worried that one of us will give it away."

Hide what? Give what away?

What was their big secret they were all afraid of him discovering?

"I'm not happy that you want to hide us from Red. He's going to have to deal, if he lives here," Gruff said.

Red stepped into the kitchen and no one said a word. Interestingly, they all looked at Harry. Why?

HARRY

His brothers looked at Harry. Their boys looked at him. Could they be any more obvious?

Harry scowled at them all, drained his cup, and stood. "Let's go look in the attic, Red."

As he stomped up the stairs, Red said, "What are you all afraid of me finding out?"

Harry didn't stop, and didn't turn around as he headed for the attic stairs.

"Harry?" Red queried. "I heard what you all said in the kitchen."

Harry huffed. He did not want to have this conversation. "Let's get in the attic and we'll talk."

The attic was a huge room, running the length of the cabin. It was stacked with trunks and boxes.

"Geez," Red muttered as he glanced around.

Harry chuckled. "My dad swore Mom was a hoarder. Now, where are my boxes?"

"Wait, first tell me what you're afraid of. I can't...I can't walk on eggshells too," Red said, quoting PJ. "It's hard enough living here as it is."

Red needed this sorted first. Harry sat down heavily on a trunk. It groaned underneath his bulk, but it didn't collapse.

"Sit down, Red."

Gingerly, Red perched on a trunk and waited.

"We're all gay," Harry said eventually. He'd never had to have this conversation before. He lived in a world where everyone knew who and what he was.

Red rolled his eyes. "I kinda worked that out. No women in the house."

Harry scowled at his sarcasm. The boy had crossed a line.

"I'm sorry. I didn't mean to be rude."

It was an apology, albeit a grudging one, and Harry gave a quick nod. It was his turn now.

"We're gay, but we're also all Daddies."

"Daddies? What do you mean?" Red frowned.

Harry sighed. "Why me?" he muttered under his breath.

"I'm glad it's you," Red said, and he looked as surprised as Harry felt. Red gave a wry smile. "I'm out of my depth here."

"You're not the only one, kid," Harry admitted. "Where do I start? A Daddy/boy relationship is a kink. You know what a kink is?" He was relieved when Red nodded. "This type of relationship is specific to gay men. We're caretakers and nurturers."

"You take care of men who've never had fathers?" Red asked.

"You'd think so, wouldn't you? But no, we've had all kinds of boys in our lives. Ones with happy families and wonderful fathers too. But since Gruff found Lyle, our life has changed."

"For your brothers who've found their...sons?"

"Boys," Harry said hastily. "Boys, not sons. But no, for all of us. We've all found new purpose and meaning." And for the first time, Harry knew he meant it, but he could see Red was still floundering. How could he make Red understand? It was hard enough for people in the lifestyle to get it, let alone a stranger. "Look. As far as the world is concerned, we're gay men and four of us have found our boyfriends, our partners. Well, Alec and Matt are...hell knows what they are. But in here, where we're safe, my brothers have found their boys, and they're very happy." Then he gave a wicked grin. "Vinny picked Damien and don't let my brother tell you any different."

"No one else knows?" Red asked dubiously.

"A lot of men know, but they're either like us or they don't care."

It was amazing how many of their friends didn't care what they got up to as long as it was safe and legal.

"Constance—"

"I don't know. You'd have to ask Lyle. But he set a metaphorical bomb across the country and now CPS is trying to keep up. He needs them, they need him. My whole family has been turned upside down." Harry fixed Red with a stare. "Me, Brad, and PJ keep the farm going so my brothers and their boys have a home to come back to. They need to know we're always here for them. If you go blabbing to social services, they'll have to investigate, and our world will be torn apart again."

"Your brothers tore *my* world apart," Red said, his voice unsteady, his eyes glistening, tears ready to fall. "Do you ever think about that?"

Harry leaned forward and placed a hand on Red's shoulder and gave it a quick squeeze. "Believe me, I know. And I wish it could have been different, but it had to be this way."

"All I wanted was to be a Greencoat." Red's voice echoed around the attic room.

Harry's heart clenched at the thought of this child growing up wanting to be evil. "Oh, kid, no. You don't want to be a Greencoat."

"They're strong and in charge."

No wonder this boy was so bitter and twisted. He had no idea what was right and what was wrong. How could he, when the only male role models in his life had been evil men?

"My brothers and I are all strong, and dominant, and not one of us would starve children or beat them or hurt them in the tower or dungeon. We're good, strong men with big hearts. That's the difference between us and Greencoats."

"If you say so." Red didn't sound convinced by Harry's speech.

Harry regarded Red, not sure what else he could say to make him understand. Then he noticed Red shiver. "Let's postpone this discussion for somewhere warmer. You need warm clothes until we can get you something new. Just don't argue, yeah? You'll need clothes wherever you go."

Red gave a grudging nod. "And Harry..."

"Yeah?"

"I don't care about you and your brothers or anyone else. It's none of my business. All I care about is being able to take care of myself."

Harry nodded, relieved Red was being pragmatic about

his bombshell. "Thanks, kid. If you give us a chance, we can help you do that."

He started to rummage through the boxes and trunks. "Everything is labeled. We need to find the boxes before we started growing into bears."

"We should try your clothes first," Red said. He blushed as Harry glanced at him. "We're both redheads. Your clothes might suit me better."

Harry groaned. "Mom didn't consider fashion and style. Everything got handed down until it was worn thin."

"It couldn't have been easy with seven boys."

"It wasn't. Money was tight. But Mom was inventive, and we managed." Harry gave a fond smile until he noticed Red's pinched expression. "I'm sorry. It must be hard for you to hear me go on about family."

"You can't miss what you didn't have," Red clearly lied, because he refused to look at Harry. "What about this box? Harry 11-12."

"Let's try it. Oh yeah, flannel shirts and Aran sweaters. I'm sorry. You're not gonna be gracing any catwalk in these."

"I don't care." Red's teeth chattered. "I'm so cold."

"Strip off your shirt and try these on," Harry ordered, handing Red a blue and red striped flannel shirt.

He tried not to notice the boy's slender body, the copper pink nipples surrounded by a little red hair, the same color as under his arms, and a dusting on his belly.

Red sighed in relief as he slipped on the shirt, then he made a grumbling noise. "It's too small."

"Let's try Harry 13-14." Harry produced another flannel shirt, green with red stripes. Red put it on, and this was a perfect fit. "Here's a green sweater too." It was a deep forest green and suited Red perfectly. "I know they smell a bit musty, but we can wash the rest of the box today if the power holds out."

"Do you have any jeans? Mine are wet."

Harry dug into the box and produced two pairs. "Try these on."

He turned his back to give Red some privacy.

"You don't have to turn around," Red said. "I'm used to changing in front of the Greencoats."

Harry stayed where he was. He heard an amused huff and then rustling sounds.

"These fit," Red said. "It's good to be warm for once."

Harry turned and smiled at Red. "Take your wet clothes and I'll take these."

He sealed the first packing case with tape left on a nearby trunk and picked up the box they were going to take downstairs. His mom would have been pleased to know his old clothes would get another chance to be worn.

"Tell me one thing about being a Daddy," Red said unexpectedly as they headed for the stairs.

"We're dominant. The boys have to do what we tell them to do."

Red gave him a wry smile. "The Greencoats told us what to do."

"There's a huge difference. We give orders with love."

"It sounds the same to me," Red muttered.

Harry shook his head. "Our boys own our hearts."

"You don't have a boy," Red said pointedly.

"Because I don't want one." Harry smiled at him. "No matter what my brothers say."

And he was going to keep saying that until they believed him. Not every Daddy needed a boy of his own. He was content to take care of the horses and spend his nights at the Tin Bar, having a little fun there.

He saw Red's expression change, and his bright eyes seemed to dim, but the kid didn't say anything as they both clattered down the stairs. Harry had been going to ask whether Red was gay. He was so unfazed by Harry's revelations. But that would have to wait for another time. At least Red would keep his family's secret safe...this time.

4

RED

The storm hit with vengeance overnight. If Red thought the wind and snow were bad before, it was nothing like the howling gale as the sun set. The wind was so strong he worried the cabin would be pushed over the mountain. None of the brothers seemed to worry about it, and Vinny and Lyle pointed out they'd lived on the mountain their whole lives. They were used to it. Even Rexy was sacked out in front of the fire, snoring loudly.

Only Red was panicking then. He said nothing about his fears, but he didn't leave Harry's side, taking comfort from his solid presence. Harry sat back in his seat, his arm casually slung across the back of Red's chair. Red wished he could push in for a cuddle as the other boys were. Lyle was on his other side, pressed into Gruff.

Harry had announced before dinner that he'd discussed his family with Red, and that Red was cool with the

Daddy/boy relationships. There wouldn't be any trouble with the authorities.

'Cool' was a relative term but Red could see the relief on their faces. It was important to them and, now that they knew, they relaxed enough to show some of the affection they hadn't before.

"It's a strong one tonight," Damien said, grimacing as the cabin seemed to rock.

"It's a good thing Jake and Aaron stayed in town," Brad agreed.

"The road's gonna be impassable," PJ said.

The brothers all grunted and Red could tell they seemed unhappy with the idea.

Lyle caught his gaze and leaned over to mutter. "The brothers like everyone to be together."

"We have co-dependency issues," Harry said, and they all agreed with him.

Red wondered how no one found it suffocating. His feelings must have been plain on his face because Lyle leaned over again and whispered in his ear.

"I like being part of a family again."

"Do you remember your parents?" Red said in a low voice.

"Barely, but my Daddy and his family make up for it."

Red looked away, unwilling to meet his gaze. He had no memories of life before the water park.

"I'm gonna take my boy to bed." Damien stood and cuddled Vinny close to him. From the beam on the young man's face, it was clear how happy he was. They left the kitchen, Rexy following hard on their heels.

Red had to swallow back the bitter taste of jealousy in the back of his throat. He couldn't remember ever being that happy.

One by one each couple disappeared upstairs until it was just PJ and Jack, plus Harry, Red, and Brad left around the kitchen table.

Brad produced a pack of cards. "Poker?"

PJ's eyes lit up and Harry nodded enthusiastically.

Red had no idea how to play poker and wasn't in the mood to learn. His skin crawled with each new crash outside. He just wanted to hide. "I think I'll go to bed. Good night."

"Night, kid," Harry said, and the others gave lazy waves. "Do you want me to come up with you?"

Red did, but he didn't want to admit it, so he shook his head and hurried to his bedroom. He jumped into bed and pulled the covers over his head, terrified by the noise. It was even worse up here than in the kitchen.

"Hey, kid. Are you okay?"

Red nearly shed his skin at the sound of Harry's voice and the bed dipping as Harry sat down.

"Red?"

He poked his head out of the covers and scowled at Harry. He hadn't heard the door open. "You scared the living crap outta me. I thought you were playing poker." No way was he showing how scared he was to anyone else.

"Dollar," Harry said automatically. "I'll pay."

"Why do you keep doing that?" Red demanded.

Harry shrugged. "Mon started the swear jar to clean up our language. Seven boys can get fruity. But we carried on because we get a nice Thanksgiving which doesn't cost us much."

Red grunted. It was really annoying.

"It's a family thing," Harry assured him. "You don't have to worry. I'll pay for you unless you curse constantly." He narrowed his eyes. "Don't even think about it."

"Like I would," Red muttered.

"You seemed worried," Harry said, changing the subject, "and I heard you crying."

"I wasn't crying," Red protested. He glowered at Harry, embarrassed that he'd been overheard.

"It's okay, kid," Harry soothed. "We're used to the storms. You're not. You can see why I ensured the animals were settled before the storm hit."

"I'm not a kid," Red grumbled, but he didn't want Harry to move away from him. "It sounds as if we're gonna take off."

Harry grinned at him. "It does, but we're solid here. This old cabin has weathered many storms. When we build the new ones, we know just how to—"

Something crashed outside. Red yelled in fright. Harry gathered Red into his arms and held him close.

"It's okay, boy. You're safe. It was probably a tree."

Red held onto Harry for dear life, burying his face in the soft hoodie. Harry was large and he made Red feel safe. He was the one constant thing in this whole mess. Red pressed his cheek against Harry's chest, listening to his steady heartbeat. Harry crooned in his ear and Red listened, but he was more focused on the feel of Harry's arms around him.

"I've got you, you're safe," Harry repeated.

Red held on tighter, hoping Harry wouldn't let go until the storm subsided. But Harry didn't seem anxious to move and Red fell asleep still wrapped in Harry's embrace, the sound of his heartbeat helping to drown out the frightening howling outside.

When he awoke the next morning, he was tucked up under the covers and Harry was gone. The storm had subsided, but when he looked out of the window, he realized no one was going anywhere. Huge snow drifts surrounded the cabin. He could barely see the barns beyond the trees. He hoped the horses were safe.

Wandering downstairs and into the kitchen, he found Lyle and Vinny in their Daddies' laps. He looked away, not wanting to intrude. He was still processing the whole Daddy/boy thing.

Lyle was being fed oatmeal and chattering about a book he'd read. Instead of leaping up to take care of Red, he glanced at Harry, who was busy scarfing down his bowl of oatmeal.

"Harry, Red needs breakfast," Gruff said.

Harry gave him a blank look. "What?"

"Red. Breakfast."

"It's okay, I'm not hungry." It wasn't true. For once Red did feel hungry, but he didn't want to cause any conflict.

Harry scowled at Gruff, but he got to his feet and beckoned Red over to the covered pan on the stove. "You have to eat something. I know it's hard to force yourself to eat at first, but I'll need your help with the horses if we can get to them, and it's hard work."

Red nodded and let Harry serve him a bowl of oatmeal. It was at least three times the size he was used to, but he'd try to eat it. He sat next to Harry at the table and took the first spoonful. It was better oatmeal than he'd been fed at the water park.

"I've told Jake and Aaron the road is blocked," Damien said suddenly. "Alec and Matt are going to meet them later. They gave up trying to get to the lead. The storm was too bad."

"At least they're safe," Gruff said, "but I'll be glad when they're home." He turned his attention to Harry. "Where were you last night? I came by your bedroom, and you weren't there."

Red held his breath, waiting for Harry to tell them he'd been crying, but Harry shrugged.

"I came down for a drink. Maybe it was then."

Gruff looked dubious. "I don't think—" Then stopped when Lyle dug him in the ribs.

"More oatmeal?" Lyle asked Red.

Red looked at his bowl. He'd barely started on this one. "No, thanks."

Gruff looked between all of them, clearly confused, but finally huffed, saying, "Don't I get seconds?"

"You eat more than all of us put together," Damien scoffed. "Except PJ. Where are he and Jack?"

"Taking advantage of a lie-in," Lyle said. "They're busy. But they're going to help dig out the drive later."

Even Red wasn't naïve enough not to know what busy meant. He focused on his breakfast and to his surprise, finished it all.

Harry smiled at him. "Good boy. Ready to help me with the horses? We're gonna have to dig through the snowdrifts."

"Yeah." He got to his feet, but Harry stopped him.

"Put the bowl in the dishwasher first."

Red flushed but he did as he was told. He found it hard to remember all the rules.

When he turned around, he found the family staring, not at him, but at Harry.

If Harry noticed, he ignored them, leading Red to the rack of coats and boots. Then he let out an explosive breath.

"I'm sorry about my family, Red. They're all really predictable."

Red stared at him, confused. "I don't understand."

Harry gave him a wry grin. "Maybe that's for the best. Now, how are you with a shovel?"

HARRY

Despite Harry's earlier misgivings, Red proved to be a hard worker. The snow was heavy, and Harry and Red struggled to clear a path through the deep drifts to the barns, but the boy worked as hard as he did. The storm had moved on, leaving drifts piled high and trees scattered on the ground, snapped like twigs against the force of the wind.

It was bitterly cold, and their gloves and hats offered little protection against the icy wind that whipped around them. Harry had made sure Red was bundled up against the cold, with solid boots, a thick jacket, hat, scarf, and gloves. They would get warm enough after the physical labor, but Red wasn't used to the cold and Harry didn't want him to get pneumonia.

Lyle scurried out as they neared the barn, holding cups of hot chocolate. He was swamped in an enormous jacket which Harry recognized as Gruff's. He hurried back to the house as soon as they'd thanked him.

"Lyle hates the snow," Harry said. "It reminds him of what could have happened."

Red nodded. "Do you live on hot chocolate?" He wanted to change the subject.

"That, and coffee," Harry agreed, taking a long swig and wiping the line of hot chocolate from his mustache. "I think Lyle just wants to check I'm not overworking you."

Red groaned as he rolled his shoulders. "I wish I'd known. I could have put in a complaint."

It was probably a joke but Harry frowned. "If it's too much, you can go inside."

They'd been working on the path for what felt like hours, taking turns to dig and clear the way. As the snow reached up to their waists in some places, the men took turns trying to break it up and shovel it away. But with each shovelful that was cleared, more snow seemed to take its place.

Red shook his head. "I like helping. It gives me time not to think." He grimaced. "I think I'm gonna need a hot shower tonight."

But he stopped for a moment, his breath visible in the air, and glanced at Harry. The look in Red's eyes was one of determination, but also one of exhaustion. Harry knew Red was running out of steam. He gazed around, trying to find a way to make their task easier, but it was easier just to push on with it.

While he shoveled, Harry mused on Red's comment about not thinking. Maybe that's what he had to do for the boy. Keep him so busy that he couldn't think about things he couldn't control, like his immediate future. He would talk to Gruff about it. He knew his little brother spent a long time with Lyle, trying to take his brain offline because his boy could never stop worrying about the fate of other boys.

The sun had just begun to peek over the horizon, and the snow sparkled like diamonds in the morning light. The air was thick with a fresh scent after a storm, and Harry could feel the warmth of the sun on his face. Despite the physical labor, he enjoyed days like this. It made him realize how much he loved living on the mountain. He would miss it when he moved away.

They reached the horses and found them in good condition. The animals whinnied in relief at the sight of the men and nuzzled them as if to say thank you.

"They're pleased to see us," Red said, a note of wonder in his voice.

"They're always excited because they think we bring treats," Harry pointed out.

Red raised one eyebrow. "And do you?" At Harry's huff, he chuckled. "Busted."

"So funny," Harry groused, but when he and Red shared a smile over Star's back as they petted her, he discovered he liked having someone to share the joke with.

He began the day's chores in the barn, grateful for his life. He remembered holding Red in the dark of the night and wondering what secrets he was hiding. But now the sun was shining, and the snow seemed to sparkle in the light. His family was safe, and even their unwilling foster kid seemed happy as he followed Harry's instructions.

Would Red weather the storm his life had become? Harry wasn't sure. For a boy determined to go his own way, he seemed vulnerable to the point he was ready to crack. Harry studied the boy as he worked. When Red left their care, Harry would ask Alec and Jake to keep tabs on him and make sure he was safe.

———

They were all exhausted by evening time. The five brothers sat around the kitchen table, Lyle and Vinny were asleep on their Daddies' laps. Jack was dozing against PJ who was half asleep himself. Harry turned to Red and grinned.

"He's asleep with his eyes open," Brad muttered.

Harry agreed with this assessment. Red's blue eyes were open but there wasn't a lot going on there.

"He worked hard today," Harry said. "I couldn't have gotten most of the work done without him. Which reminds me, one corner of the barn near Thunder's stall is damaged. We'll need to repair it."

Brad grunted. "Get the lumber and I'll do it. They're forecasting more storms, so the sooner the better."

"We could get Alec and Jake to bring it up," Harry suggested, then he caught Brad's disgusted expression and chuckled.

Jake and Alec were great PIs, but not much good at the practical side of running the farm. They helped when they were asked to, and especially in late Fall, early winter, when they sold the Christmas trees, but Brad had a lot of uncomplimentary comments about Jake and his use of power tools.

"I'll drive down when the road is clear," Harry said.

"You could take your boy with you," Brad suggested. "Give him time off the mountain."

"That's a great idea. We could both do with a break." Harry lunged as Red slid the opposite way and hauled him upright, tight against his side to stop him from falling over. Red didn't stir. "I think he needs to go to bed."

Brad didn't bother to hide his amused expression. "You'd better take him upstairs." He laughed openly as Harry scowled at him. "You were the one who caught him."

"Don't get any ideas," Harry warned.

"Would I?"

Harry stood and picked Red up. Red curled into him, burying his face into Harry's neck. Harry sighed at the amused, yet satisfied looks from his brothers. "Don't get any ideas," he repeated.

"You look good together," Damien rumbled.

PJ opened his mouth.

"Don't even think about it," Harry warned.

PJ's look of innocence was wholly fake. Harry knew his brother only too well. But PJ kept quiet. It might have been the warning nod from Damien or the sleepy kiss from Jack. Harry wasn't sure which.

Harry carried Red up the stairs and into the little

bedroom. All the boys had started in this tiny room, except Lyle, whose room had been turned into a playroom for the boys.

It was like a halfway point before they got accepted into the family. Except Red was different. He didn't want to stay here. Harry felt a pang as he juggled Red, pulling back the covers and laying him down. Red was dressed in a long-sleeved T-shirt and sweats, as his clothes from earlier had been soaked through. He could sleep in these.

Harry tucked him under the covers and Red snuggled in with a relieved sigh. His copper-bright lashes were very dark against the pale skin of his cheeks. He was beautiful, Harry was sure of that.

He hoped Red would find someone to take care of him when he left the farm. He bent over and pushed Red's hair back from his face.

"Don't trust anyone, little one," he whispered. "Not until you know they're the right person to give your heart to. You're all bravado and bluster but under there…" He touched Red's heart. "You're a sweet boy desperate to be loved. It's so obvious."

Harry reached the door when Red spoke.

"I don't trust anyone, Harry. It's what's kept me alive."

He turned to face Red, but the kid still had his eyes closed. "That's not what I said."

"But it's the only thing that's true."

"No, my boy, it isn't."

"For me, it is. Night, Harry." Red turned over to face the wall. The conversation was over.

Harry hesitated, then his heart cracked as he left the bedroom. Red would never survive in the outside world. How could Harry keep him safe?

5

RED

The silence outside penetrated Red's dreams. He opened one eye and looked at the bedroom door, but it was closed. He kicked off the covers and rolled over onto his back, still finding it too hot in his bedroom after years of sleeping in drafty dorm rooms. He stared up at the ceiling and sighed. It was early, although he'd heard the brothers get up hours before. Red had closed his eyes after they trampled downstairs and fallen back to sleep. As they went to bed the previous night, Harry had told Red to sleep in after days of hard work. Red didn't object. He was exhausted and glad of the extra rest.

He'd been at the cabin for a week already. The storm was long gone and yet he was still there. There were good reasons he hadn't left. The storm had been stronger than expected and for a few days, the mountain road was impassable.

At first, Red was worried they didn't have enough food, but Harry had shown him the barn full of freezers. The

Brenners had enough food to last an apocalypse or at least a zombie invasion. He'd seen a movie about invading zombies. The humans never seemed to be prepared.

Harry laughed when Red told him that. "Seven large men eat more than you think, but we're always prepared for bad weather. And since Lyle arrived, we have had more men joining us and a lot of guests. But we never worry about food…unless Brad blows up this barn."

This was an ongoing joke among the family he didn't understand. If someone did that in the water park, they'd have been arrested. Here, they just laughed about it. Brad seemed normal enough apart from that. Red paused in his thoughts. As normal as being part of seven gay Daddy bears could be.

Finally, the mountain road was open, and Jake and Aaron had returned home, while Alec and Matt were still chasing a lead. From what Red had gathered, Alec and Jake swapped times to be at home now.

He didn't really care. It was time Red moved on. He just couldn't cope with all the brothers and the whole loving family bullshit, which was why he spent most of his time with the horses. It was easier. It was hard work and most of the time he ate, worked, and collapsed into bed without having to think.

The whole Daddy/boy thing was starting to wear on him. But that wasn't the main reason. No, the main issue was the red-headed bear who spent too much time inhabiting Red's dreams.

The week had been a long one. Red watched all the boys sit with their Daddies and, even though he wasn't a boy, he really wasn't, images of him sitting on Harry's lap, being loved and cared for, played out in his head as he tried to ignore them.

It was beyond anything he'd known before. Red had had crushes, and even considered himself in love with one of the Greencoats once. That had lasted until the man had taken a chosen. Red had told himself not to waste time on a lost cause. Crushes were normal. He knew that from listening to the older boys talking in his dorm. But his feelings had been fleeting and they didn't last.

Harry was a different matter. Red was developing feelings for Harry, though he knew he shouldn't. Harry had been kind and taken care of him, made sure he had something to eat and drink, even when Red didn't want anything. He didn't seem to mind that Red wanted to spend all his time outside except when it was mealtimes, because Harry did that too.

They'd spent almost the whole week in each other's company, Harry training him how to take care of the sweet-natured mares, standing behind him, showing him how to groom them, with Red acutely aware of Harry's strong body behind him. It was driving Red wild and there was nothing he could do about it. He wanted to push Harry into the barn wall and kiss him. But he couldn't do that. He never did that. Red kept his head down and never let anyone see his true feelings. Just like he'd always done. Because that was what kept him alive.

Red sucked in a breath. It didn't matter what he wanted or what Harry wanted. Leaving was the best thing he could do. He clambered out of bed and into a T-shirt and jeans, and a hoodie. He sat down to roll on thick socks and shoved his feet into old slippers Harry had found for him.

Then he sighed and buried his face in his hands. He was dressed head to toe in clothes Harry had found for him. He felt as if he were wrapped up in Harry's arms, just wearing his old clothes.

It was time he moved on. There was only one thing he needed. His birth certificate and any other details about his family. Lyle had promised to obtain them, but it took time. Too much time.

Red took a deep breath, opened his bedroom door, stomped downstairs past the elephant poop picture, and into the kitchen. Harry was nowhere to be seen. There was only Lyle, Vinny, and Damien in the kitchen.

"Morning, Red," Lyle said, smiling at him as he stirred something in a pan. From the sweet smell, it was the ever-present pan of hot chocolate. "Do you want oatmeal, there's still some left, or something cooked?"

"Oatmeal is fine, thank you," Red said, although he wasn't hungry. He wished they wouldn't push food on him all the time.

Lyle nodded. "Sit down at the table."

Red hesitated, not wanting to sit with Damien and Vinny, then he headed over to the stove.

"It's okay, I can heat the oatmeal," Lyle said, chuckling at him.

Red shook his head. "It's not that. I wanted to talk to you about something. You know I need my papers. Have you tracked them down yet?"

"Yeah, we haven't had a chance to look for your birth certificate yet, Red." Lyle shot him an apologetic smile. "I'm sorry. It's been kind of busy around here, between the theme parks and the storm."

"But you promised," Red managed as calmly as he could.

"I know, and I will get around to it. I'm just trying to handle a lot at the moment."

Get around to it? Was he fucking kidding?

Red just stared at him, unable to believe what he'd just

heard. If he spent less time making hot chocolate and sitting on Gruff's lap and more time doing his damn job, Red wouldn't be stuck here waiting.

"I can't leave until you find my birth certificate," he pointed out. "You promised to help me."

Lyle shrugged, then spooned oatmeal into a bowl. "I don't know what you expect me to do, Red. We're working as fast as we can. You know how busy we've been."

Silence fell over the kitchen. Red heard the *drip, drip* from the faucet in the kitchen sink. He could smell the cinnamon in the hot chocolate. He was aware of all eyes on him. All his senses were on high alert.

He felt the bitter taste of betrayal in the back of his throat. Why did he think these men were going to be any different from the Greencoats who had controlled his entire life? This was another prison and, unlike Kingdom theme parks, he had no idea when he'd be out of here.

Red felt the pressure building behind his eyes. He clenched his fists, trying to keep control.

"I want to go back to the water park."

"You can't do that, Red," Lyle said gently. "You know that. It's closed for good."

"It's my home."

"Not now, Red. This is your home."

HARRY

Harry and PJ had barely opened the door when Red shouted.

"I hate you!"

Harry heard the heartfelt "Feeling reciprocated, kid," behind him. PJ did not like their newest foster boy. PJ was also missing his boy which had a lot to do with it. Aaron and Jack had decided to have a couple of days in town, meeting up with friends from the bar, and PJ wasn't coping with the separation. But they weren't the ones being yelled at. No, Harry was sure that pleasure was aimed at Lyle.

Harry had come from the stables, PJ from the farm. Making eye contact, they shed their coats and hats and silently agreed to hide in the hall until the tantrum was over. Lyle was much better at handling Red in a snit than they were, although Harry knew he was being a coward.

"I don' wanna stay here anymore." The volume hadn't decreased.

Lyle was clearly at the end of his patience with Red from the tight edge to his voice. "Red, you have to stay for now. You're not eighteen yet."

"You don't know that," Red snapped. "I could be twenty-one."

"Or twelve," PJ muttered.

Harry gave his brother a quick grin. Red's behavior was very reminiscent of him and his brothers in their early years.

"You didn't get disappeared, kid," Damien pointed out. "You can't be eighteen yet."

"It was coming though," Red muttered. "The Greencoats kept talking about it."

Harry and PJ exchanged glances. It was the first time Red had admitted that. It meant the Greencoats knew.

"Maybe Alec and Jake could speak to one of the Greencoats," PJ whispered in Harry's ear. "Then we can send him on his way."

"Give him a chance," Harry muttered, huffing when PJ made a derisive snort.

"But we don't know," Lyle said gently from the kitchen.

"We can't find your records, which makes you our responsibility until we see your birth certificate."

"You can't keep me locked up here."

"It's not a prison, kid." That was Damien.

"And you can fuck off too," Red snapped.

"Oooh no." Harry closed his eyes and PJ groaned loudly. Big mistake. *Big* mistake.

3...2...1...

"Don't you dare yell at my Daddy!" Vinny bellowed.

For a boy the size of a half pint, he had a set of lungs on him.

"Vinny, it's okay," Damien said soothingly.

"No. It's not okay. He doesn't get to behave like an asshole—sorry, Lyle—to either of you. But especially not you. You need to get the hell over yourself, Red."

"Vinny's gonna kill him," PJ murmured.

Harry caught PJ's expectant look. "What?"

"Go deal with your boy."

"He's not my boy."

PJ rolled his eyes. "Yeah, he is. And you need to deal with him before he gets out of hand. More out of hand," he added, in case it wasn't clear. "Lyle doesn't deserve this."

Great, now Harry felt guilty because he also knew Lyle didn't deserve any of this shit. He glared at PJ. "Just because he works in the stables does not make him my boy."

"Then whose is he?"

"I don't care. He's not mine. I don't want a boy."

PJ shrugged. "He needs a Daddy to take him in hand. You're it."

Harry glowered, but PJ ignored him and headed into the danger zone.

"Where's my hot chocolate?" he bellowed.

Harry followed reluctantly, knowing if he made a bolt

for it, PJ would haul him back. Harry was huge, but PJ was built like the side of a barn. Harry wouldn't get far. He wondered how he was going to get out of this situation.

The thing was, not every boy wanted to be rescued. Not every Daddy was ready to take care of a boy. But Harry was learning fast that not everyone got what they wanted.

It was easy to see the relief on everyone's faces when they spotted Harry. Everyone except Red, who just glared at him. They all expected him to take Red in hand.

Damien sat at the table, Vinny on his lap. Lyle and Red faced off by the stove. PJ ignored them all and pushed past Red to access the pan on the stovetop which Lyle had been stirring, ready for their morning break. No one was going to get between PJ and his chocolate.

Harry took a deep breath and looked at Lyle. "Problems?"

Lyle looked bruised and battered by the confrontation with Red. "Red wants to go back to Kingdom Water Park."

The boy was wearing him down, wearing on all of them, but Lyle in particular. Gruff's boy had the heart of a lion and he tried to take on the problems of all the boys he rescued. The trouble was they had never come across one who wanted to go back to the prison he had been in.

Harry pinned Red with a glare. "The water park is closed. You know that."

Red scowled at him. "I can live there on my own."

"No, you can't," Harry said flatly. "You know that too. If you can't be polite, go back to the stables. Star needs exercising."

"I'm not your servant."

"You're living here, and you do your chores like every other member of the family."

"I'm not part of the family," Red snapped.

That's your choice, kid. But Harry didn't say it out loud.

He folded his arms across his chest and scowled at the boy. "I don't care. You live here which makes you one of us and you obey our rules."

Someone crowed under his breath. PJ. It had to be him. Harry ignored him, his attention focused on Red. The boy had to realize he was treading on very thin ice here.

"You obeyed the rules at the water park. You obey ours."

"It's just another prison," Red burst out.

"For heaven's sake, it's nothing like a prison." Lyle threw his hands up in the air. "You're not beaten. You get three meals a day. Or you would, if you ate anything. You sleep in a bed, you have your own room."

"And I hate it!" Red yelled. "I'm so alone."

He fled out of the kitchen, leaving everyone staring at each other.

Gruff suddenly appeared in the doorway. "What's wrong with Red? Did I miss something? I heard yelling."

Lyle hurried over and buried himself against Gruff's chest. Gruff hugged him in his meaty arms. "Red's upset."

"He's alone and scared," Vinny said, surprising Harry. "He's lost all the structure that made up his day, all the boys that were his friends. He's an asshole because he's so frightened."

Damien sighed and pulled a dollar out of his pocket to put in the swear jar.

"Three dollars," PJ pointed out. "Your boy swore twice before."

PJ was always keen to point out transgressions as he was the one who filled the swear jar the most.

Vinny kissed his cheek. "Sorry, Daddy."

"Don't do it again," Damien grumbled as he added another two dollars.

"But Vinny's right," Lyle admitted. "When I arrived, I did the chores. I was used to that. Vinny did the same. Aaron and Jack worked."

"Red's helped me in the stables," Harry pointed out. "He's worked real hard and he's happy out there."

Lyle nodded. "Because he's not in here. He hates it in here with us."

"What did he do at the water park?" Damien asked.

"He handled the money. He said he's good at math. Not so good at English."

Damien grunted. "He could help with the family accounts."

Vinny scowled at him. "Does that mean he spends time with you?"

"We'll work it out," Damien promised.

"He could help me with the stock take," Brad suggested. "I could teach him chemistry if he doesn't try to blow us up. That's got math."

Harry nodded. "We could all find work for him. Finding work is not the problem. The point is, what does he want to do?"

"You better ask him, little brother," Brad said.

"He's not my boy," Harry repeated for the hundredth time, knowing it was futile.

"But he listens to you."

Harry snorted. "He yells at me."

"He yells at all of us," Gruff said. "But he listens to *you*. And right now, you're the only thing keeping him from flying apart. So he's your responsibility."

"I don't want—"

"Tough," Damien said. "It's your turn, little brother. A boy needs you and you've got to step up."

"Are you a Daddy or a mouse?" Gruff said.

Harry furrowed his brow. "What does that even mean?"

Damien chuckled. "He said it to me too. It still doesn't make sense. But what are you? A Daddy doesn't let a boy fall apart. Red needs you. He might not be your forever boy, but he's the boy here in front of you. Now help him."

Faced with the resolute expressions from his brothers, and the frankly pleading expression from Lyle, Harry knew he was backed into a corner. Damien was right. He couldn't turn away a boy in need, even if the boy didn't want to be helped.

Fuck!

"A dollar," PJ said.

Harry gaped at him. "I didn't say anything."

"You cursed. I saw the look."

"He's right," Brad agreed. "You definitely swore."

"I'll put it in when I get back," Harry snapped. "I might hafta put more in then. And I want hot chocolate."

"I'll fill two travel cups," Lyle said, hurrying to the cabinet. "Red was too busy yelling to have breakfast."

Harry shrugged his coat on and jammed his hat on his head, then stomped into his boots.

Lyle handed him the cups. "He doesn't mean to be so rude."

Harry shook his head. "Don't make excuses for him, Lyle. He's scared and unhappy, but that doesn't give him the right to be rude, especially to you."

Lyle gave him a rueful look. "It's easier to be rude to me. He knows I won't punish him. You guys he's not so sure about. You're more like Greencoats."

Harry was offended by that comparison. He and his brothers were *nothing* like Greencoats.

"Sorry." Lyle grimaced.

"Why does my boy have to apologize?" Gruff said, wrapping a beefy arm around Lyle's thin shoulders.

"He called us Greencoats."

"You didn't have to tell him," Lyle hissed. "Traitor."

"You called me a Greencoat," Harry pointed out. He took a deep breath. "You know, you had the poisoned apple, Aaron was locked up like Rapunzel, Damien thought he was the ugly duckling, and Jack had the beans. What the heck is Red and me?" He caught their 'what the hell' expressions. "What?"

"Your boy is called Red," Gruff pointed out.

"Yeah?"

"Oh, come on." Gruff huffed at Harry's clueless stare. "Red Riding Hood? You remember that one?"

Harry gave him a flat stare. "I'm not the granny or the wolf."

"You haven't finished the story yet. Now go before the hot chocolate is cold." Lyle shooed him out the door.

"I'm not the granny," Harry yelled.

The door closed on their mocking laughter.

"I'm not the granny," he muttered, stomping toward the stable, "and I'm definitely not a wolf."

But he was ready to go all Daddy Bear on a certain boy's ass.

6

RED

Steaming with rage, Red kicked at the snow and the gravel, sending it flying across the path on his way to the barn. Lyle was wrong. It was just another prison. Like the other four homes had been. None of them had been willing to give him any freedom. At least with the other foster homes, he'd been able to run away, even if he had been caught. Here he was trapped.

And Lyle should have been the one to understand how he felt, but he didn't care. He was more interested in being fed by his Daddy than in Red's turmoil.

He'd been stupid to be rude to Damien. He didn't care about Damien being angry. In the time he'd been here, Red had realized Damien could get grumpy, but he was soft and sweet like cotton candy inside. No, it was Vinny who was the scary one. He was so overprotective of Damien.

"I hate you all," Red muttered and lashed out at the snow again.

He was frustrated and angry at being trapped here,

annoyed that Harry was barking orders at him in front of everyone when he'd considered Harry was his one ally, but more to the point he was embarrassed at himself. He had never meant to lose his temper like that.

"Red, wait up."

Dammit! What did Jack want?

He turned to see Jack and Aaron hurrying toward him.

Just peachy. Now there were two more of them.

He hadn't had much to do with either of the boys. Aaron had been trapped in the town until the mountain road cleared and Jack was elusive, preferring to stay in his bedroom or with PJ.

"What do you want?"

"Look, we overheard your fight in the kitchen," Aaron said. "We just wanted you to know you can talk to us if you want."

"Why would I want to talk to you?" he snapped.

"Because we're the newest ones here," Jack said, "and we understand how overwhelming it can be becoming part of this family."

Red gritted his teeth. "I'm not part of the family."

Jack nodded and there didn't seem to be any judgment. "You don't have to be with a brother to be part of the family. Look at Matt. Oh, have you met him?"

"Briefly. I thought he was with Alec."

Aaron barked out a laugh. "Not officially, and not in Matt's eyes. The rest of us are just waiting for him to wake the hell up. The point is, Red, take a deep breath and let Jake and Alec find out who you are and how old you are. There are worse places to be."

"How would you know?" Red snapped. "You're not from a Kingdom park."

Aaron grimaced. "There are other prisons in the world. My mom locked me up for thirteen years until I escaped."

"And my uncle abused me," Jack added. "We've all had our trauma. You're not the only one to have suffered."

"I didn't suffer," Red muttered. "I liked it at the water park. It's all I know."

"You weren't treated badly like Lyle or Vinny?" Jack asked curiously.

Red shrugged. "It could have been worse. I was beaten when I misbehaved."

"But it's got to be better here," Aaron said.

"Why?" Red demanded. "Because I get food and a bed? I had somewhere to sleep before. This is just another place where I have to do what I'm told. What's the difference? I just want to go home."

"You've got a whole family who wants to take care of you." Aaron was gentle enough but Red could see he didn't understand.

Red shook his head fiercely. "No. I'm here because I had nowhere else to go. You don't want me here."

"Get over yourself, kid," Jack snapped. "Lyle was found almost dead in the snow. Vinny was beaten continuously. Aaron was beaten up and left for dead on the side of the road. I ran away from my uncle. The Brenners took us in. They didn't have to, but they've got big hearts."

"I don't want to be here," Red said furiously. How many times did he have to repeat it?

"The second we know you're eighteen, you can walk out the gate." A new voice behind him. Harry.

Red closed his eyes. He opened them to see two smirking faces. He scowled but their smirks grew wider.

"We'll leave you to it," Aaron said, and Jack nodded.

They hurried away, leaving Red staring after them.

"I thought those two were out for the rest of the day," Harry muttered. "At least PJ's temper will improve now."

Red turned to face him and folded his arms across his chest. "Go on then."

Harry looked confused. "Go on then, what?"

"Give me the lecture."

"What lecture?"

Red huffed. "You've come after me. You've got a lecture."

"No lecture, I promise. I do have hot chocolate though." Harry reached into his coat and pulled out a cup with a lid. "Drink it now."

Red stared at him, bewildered. "No lecture?"

Harry handed him the cup and pulled out another one. "Listen, kid. I know you don't want to hear what everyone is saying to you, but that's your choice. I can't make you listen. Just drink up. Then we've got work to do." He took a long slug from the cup. "Yeah, drink up. It's just right now."

Red did as he was told. He didn't know what else to do. He took a sip. Harry was right. The hot chocolate was perfect. It was about the only thing he liked about being here. Except maybe the bed. He was getting used to that. And being warm. Except now. Now he was freezing.

And maybe Harry. Harry was good to him. Maybe he liked Harry most of all. He looked up to see Harry watching him closely.

"What?" he asked, all defensive now.

"Feeling better?" Harry asked, his tone gentle.

Red nodded, pressing his lips together, and hiding the sudden tears in his eyes. He hated feeling so vulnerable. He'd spent his whole life keeping his head down and now he was exposed. He focused on finishing the hot chocolate before it was cold.

"I need to get supplies in town. Do you want to come with me?"

Red looked at Harry, narrowing his eyes. "You mean it? This isn't some kind of test?"

Harry rolled his eyes. "It's not a test, kid. You feel trapped and I've got to visit the lumber merchants. We're due another storm and the barn needs repairs. Brad has promised to do it if I get the timber."

"And you don't think I'm gonna run away?"

Harry shrugged. "If you do, I ain't hunting for you, kid. I've got a busy day ahead and I could do with the company and the help. It's up to you."

Excitement bubbled through Red at the thought of doing something normal, like 'outside' people did, but he just gave a curt nod. "I'll come."

"We'll eat in town. I'd take you to the bar but you're not old enough, so I'll take you to the diner." Harry looked genuinely pleased with Red's acceptance. "You take the cups back to the kitchen and I'll warm up the truck." He wrinkled his nose. "It's a bucket of rust so don't expect a comfy ride."

Red bit back a grin. "I realized that the other day," he said solemnly.

Harry chuckled. "Listen, if you're scared of the height, just close your eyes and listen to the music."

"Thanks." Red appreciated the thought.

"Can you drive?"

"Not down the mountain road," Red admitted. "But I had to drive vehicles in the waterpark."

Harry nodded. "Lyle said it was a huge place. Do you have a license?"

"What's a license?" Red asked.

"That's top of the list," Harry said. "Once we discover your identity."

"We could use a fake identity," Red suggested.

"Nice try, kid. Isn't gonna happen. Do you know how many cops and Feds we deal with now? Come on, we need to go, or it'll be dark before we get to town. Cups in the kitchen. I'll meet you at the truck."

Returning to the kitchen wasn't on top of Red's things he wanted to do list, especially after he'd stormed out—again. But he was going to have to go in there at some point.

He took Harry's cup, held his head up high, and stalked back to the cabin. He could do this. He headed for the kitchen door, surprised to find it open. Red paused on the threshold as he heard Lyle's quiet voice.

"What if you can't find it, Alec? Red deserves to know the truth. We can't hide it from him forever."

"One more chance, Lyle. Matt and me, we've got an idea. If not, then I'm gonna ask Josh Cooper for his help." Alec's voice sounded tinny, as if he were on speaker.

"Do *not* introduce Red to Josh Cooper. Geez. We'll never survive the fallout."

Red stepped into the kitchen and all eyes locked on him. He saw Gruff facepalm and Lyle groaned.

"Busted," Red said without a trace of humor.

"Red, I guess you heard all that," Lyle said.

"I did. What're you hiding from me?"

"Vinny, get Harry," Damien muttered, low, but not low enough.

"He's at his truck," Red snapped. "Now talk."

"I've messaged him," Gruff said.

"I'll do it," Alec said. "Red, we can't find any trace of you. Not when you were handed to the orphanage, or your birth certificate. Nothing. As far as the world is concerned, you don't exist."

"I wasn't ignoring you, Red," Lyle said. "I just didn't have anything to tell you."

"What the hell," Harry roared as he burst into the kitchen. "You couldn't wait until I got here to deliver the news?"

Red turned on him, ready to feel betrayed. "You knew?"

"No, I just heard what he said."

"Harry's telling the truth. He didn't know." Lyle jumped in. "The only ones who knew there was a problem were Alec, Jake, and me."

Harry rushed over to Red's side. "I promise you, I didn't know. I would have told you otherwise."

Red just stood there, his feet rooted to the floor, unable to process his next thought beyond he didn't exist in the world.

"Boy, look at me." Harry stepped into his space, cupped his chin, and made him look up.

"Who am I?" Red whispered, locking gazes with Harry's blue eyes. Then Harry blurred as tears filled his eyes. "Who the hell am I?"

HARRY

Without thinking, Harry pulled Red into his arms and turned him so he was shielded from the rest of the room. He held on tight as Red shook in his arms. The boy didn't resist, instead, he hung on, seemingly needing the comfort.

"I've got you. I won't let you go until you're ready," he murmured.

It felt as if the boy would fly apart unless he held him tight. He could hear Lyle and Gruff talking with Alec in the background, but he didn't pay any attention to them, his whole focus on Red. Whatever happened with the kid, he had to know someone had his back.

"Red, you're not alone. We'll find out who you are. Alec and Jake are the best."

To be honest, Harry didn't know if they could handle something like this, but he would walk to the ends of the earth for his brothers, and he knew they would do the same. The same went for everyone in the household, including Red. They wouldn't let him down.

"I could just walk off the side of the mountain and no one would care," Red sobbed.

Harry held on tighter. "Don't say that."

"But it's true." Red sobbed harder. "You took it all away from me. I knew who I was, and you took it away."

"You're still you, Red," Harry insisted.

Red shook his head. "I just want to go back to the way things were."

"Life changes, Red." Harry settled Red more comfortably in his arms. "It's one of the things you learn as you grow up. You've got to get used to a new life. You can't go back to the way things were before. It would have changed in the water park when you reached eighteen." He didn't want to be blunt, but it had to be said. "You would have been chosen or disappeared."

"No," Red said brokenly.

"Yes, you know this. It happened to all the children."

"That's not true. Boys left and found new jobs."

"No, they didn't," Lyle said, his voice quiet, as he stepped closer to them. "I know you don't want to hear this, Red, but we found out what happened to some of the missing boys. I didn't tell you because I didn't want to upset you."

Harry felt Red's sudden hitch of his breath. Then Red wiped his eyes with the back of his hand and stepped out of Harry's embrace. Harry let him go, but stayed close in case he was needed again.

"Tell me," Red demanded.

"They were taken to the Everglades."

"You're lying!" Red yelled, his expression horrified.

Lyle shook his head. "I'm not lying. One of the Green-coats told us. You know I'm not lying. You might not want to believe it, but it's true."

"It is true," Alec said. "I spoke to two other Greencoats who confirmed it. None of the disappeared survived. They couldn't risk it getting out."

Harry had forgotten his brother was on speakerphone. "What are the Everglades?"

"It's a national park," Lyle said. "A wetland. It's full of alligators."

Harry's stomach turned over as he realized the implica-tion. "Fuck." He dug out the dollar and shoved it in the swear jar before anyone could say anything.

"They promised..." The blood drained from Red's face, and he clamped his hand over his mouth. "Gonna—"

Harry hoisted him up and headed for the outside as it was the closest. Red bent over and retched the second Harry let him go.

"I've got you, boy," he crooned, rubbing soothing circles on his back, waiting for Red to puke up his fear and anger and sadness.

Lyle appeared in the doorway and handed Harry a bottle of water. "I'm sorry. I shouldn't have told him. It's too much."

Harry nodded, but he didn't have time to focus on Lyle, because Red straightened. Harry uncapped the water and

Red drained it dry. There was a moment when Harry wasn't sure if the water was about to make a reappearance, then Red took a deep breath and focused on Lyle.

"This is true? Everything you just told me?"

"Yes," Lyle said sadly.

"That's what the Greencoats would have done to me?" Red demanded.

"If you weren't chosen, yes."

Red spat on the snow, but thankfully away from Harry and Lyle. "And they did the same to you?"

"We were sedated and turned out into the snow to freeze to death."

"I found more than one body on our land," Harry admitted. "We thought they were hikers who'd lost their way."

"And elsewhere?"

"All the parks were the same," Lyle said. "Every single one had their own method for getting rid of the disappeared. I'm not going to tell you how. I dream about it, night after night."

Harry narrowed his eyes at Lyle who had the grace to look embarrassed. "You should have told me. Have you told Gruff?"

"He hasn't, but I guessed," Gruff rumbled, appearing behind him. "I'll make sure he talks to you soon."

"Real soon," Harry insisted, "I mean it. And anyone else who needs me."

"I think *he* does," Gruff said, nodding at Red, and pulled Lyle back into the kitchen.

Harry turned to Red who stared off into the distance, his eyes unfocused and expression distraught. He hauled Red into his arms and held him tight. "I'm here, Red. You can lean on me."

"I knew, I knew," Red whispered. "But I didn't want to believe it."

"Even if you could go back, I wouldn't let you take one foot inside that hellhole," Harry said.

Red sighed and leaned against him. "I would never have been chosen."

"You wouldn't?" Harry said it cautiously, not sure where this was going. Red had never spoken about his time in the water park, other than he wanted to be back there.

"I kept my head down. I was quiet. I didn't cause trouble. I was ignored most of the time. I doubt most of the Greencoats knew I existed." He scowled at Harry's snort. "What was that for?"

"The idea of you being quiet."

"I thought being quiet would save me from being chosen."

Harry sucked in a breath at Red's frankness. "You didn't want to be chosen by the Greencoats?"

"No, never. They were old or vicious or both. No one wanted to be chosen by the Greencoats. The only ones who were chosen wanted to be Greencoats themselves. I wanted to become one, but I knew it was impossible. When my friends were disappeared, it was a relief. I knew, I hoped, they were free, you know? I had no idea what happened to them. Now they don't exist, and no one will remember them."

Harry stroked Red's hair, now sodden with sweat. The boy needed a shower. "*You'll* remember them. Maybe, if you feel you could do this, you could sit down, and we could write about them."

He thought about what he'd just said for a moment. Maybe that was a project including Lyle and Vinny too.

"I'd like that," Red admitted, "although I don't think my writing is good enough."

"We could use speech-to-text software." Harry saw Red's confused expression. "Don't worry. I'll explain later. Let's go inside. It's cold and you need a shower."

"Don't you want to go into town?" Red chewed on his bottom lip. "I think I'm too tired."

Harry knew what an admission that had to be for him. "We'll go tomorrow morning. We'll still have time to do the repairs before the next storm."

He guided Red inside, the heat welcome after the bone-chilling cold of the outside. The kitchen was empty.

Red shivered, saying, "I'm sorry."

"Nothing to apologize for," Harry said.

Without thinking, he stripped off Red's coat for him, then his own, and guided him into the hallway to hang them on the hooks and stow their boots.

"Do you want a drink?" Harry asked. "Chocolate or soda?" Red didn't drink coffee.

Red shook his head. "I just want to shower and sleep. I don't even want to process."

Harry led him upstairs, but instead of taking him to the small room, he guided Red into his bedroom.

"The shower is better in here than the family bathroom. Ignore the mess. I don't spend much time in here."

His brothers who were now in relationships had made their rooms into more private quarters, whereas Harry and Brad were either outside or in the kitchen. There was talk of them building cabins for each couple, and they'd drawn plans and plotted out spaces on the farm, but somehow it never happened, and they all stayed in the main cabin so they could be close together.

Red nodded and yawned. He was wiped out, his shoulders slumped, and the fire had gone from his eyes. The past hour had knocked the life from him.

Harry put an arm around his shoulders and led him to the bathroom. He turned on the water. "Give it a minute to heat up. I'll fetch you a towel."

When he returned Red hadn't moved. Harry wasn't sure Red was even awake. He hesitated, then he said, "I could shower you, if you want help?"

7

"I'm not..." Red started, then trailed off. He wasn't. Not at all. And Harry needed to know this. "I'm so tired."

But Harry nodded as if he understood. " Let me help. We'll keep our briefs on. I won't touch you inappropriately."

"I don't want a Daddy." He was going to make that clear from the start, but Harry nodded and smiled.

Red sighed. Harry was so easy to be around compared to his brothers.

"I don't want a boy," Harry said. "It's all good."

"I just need to make it clear," Red insisted.

"It's crystal clear, kid. Come on, let's get you undressed, or we'll waste all the hot water."

Red stood while Harry undressed him, then let himself be steered into the shower. The feel of the hot water pounding on his shoulders was wonderful.

He yelped when Harry squeezed in behind him. "What the—?" He turned to catch a big bear of a man covered in red fur. Yeah, Harry was red all over, just like he was.

"What are you doing in here?"

"I can't wash you if I'm standing outside the shower, can I? Besides I smell of horses and vomit. Not a winning combination." Harry picked up the shampoo bottle. "Close your eyes and I'll wash your hair."

Red was glad his back was to Harry as he blushed, from head to foot. It was ridiculous. He'd shared showers many times with other boys. But that was the point. They were boys, not men. And Harry was all man. Red's dick knew it only too well.

"You know I can wash myself," he muttered, willing his dick to subside. It didn't seem to be listening.

"Shut up and close your eyes," Harry said briskly.

Red closed his eyes and prayed this would be over quickly. Harry gave him as much space as possible, which Red appreciated, but every so often Red would feel the hard, furry chest and belly brush his back as Harry moved.

"You really are a bear," he muttered, but Harry didn't seem to hear him.

The way Harry stroked the aromatic shampoo through his hair was wonderful. Then he directed Red under the spray and repeated the process with something called conditioner.

Red had no idea what it was, he just did as he was told. He groaned as Harry's wicked fingers massaged his scalp. "Tell me someone trained you to do that."

"YouTube is a wonderful thing."

"What's YouTube?"

Harry chuckled behind him. "You know, after Lyle and Vinny, nothing much should surprise me about the lives you boys led, but it always does. When we get out, we'll go on my laptop, and I'll show you the wonders of YouTube. Stick your head under the water to rinse out the conditioner."

Red grunted, intrigued, and did as he was told, but he had other things on his mind.

"Can you tell how old I am?"

Harry hummed as he picked up another bottle. "Maybe if a doctor examined you, but I doubt they'd be able to put an exact age on you. You're not like a tree. You don't have rings. You're obviously young, more Lyle's and Vinny's age than me or my brothers. Are you still growing?"

"No, I haven't gotten any taller for a couple of years."

"So you've reached your maximum height. About five-nine, I'd guess." Harry huffed. "You could be anything from sixteen to twenty-one. You say the Greencoats were talking about you leaving?"

"Yes."

"So more the younger to middle end, then. I'm going to wash your back and shoulders."

Washing Red's back and shoulders was fine. It turned into another massage, which Red appreciated. Red sighed as Harry's firm hands stroked down his spine.

"That's not my back." Red's voice cracked.

"Nope, done that." Harry was now on his knees washing Red's thighs and down his legs.

"I can do my front," Red insisted.

"Okay. Hold out your hand."

Harry squeezed a large puddle of amber gel into Red's palm. Then he did the same and started washing his chest.

Flushing again, Red turned away and washed his face, chest, and groin, sudden images of Harry's hand on his cock and balls playing out in his mind.

No! He had to push those thoughts away. Keeping his

head down and not getting involved with anyone was what kept him alive.

"Red? Is everything all right?" Harry sounded concerned.

"Yeah, why?"

"You stopped breathing."

"I'm fine," Red lied.

Then Harry turned Red to face him and Red found himself confronted with a furry chest. He focused on the spray of freckles on Harry's shoulders. Harry cupped Red's jaw and made him look up. "I know when you're lying. Tell me what's wrong."

"I'm not used to...this." Red waved his hand, trying not to touch any part of Harry.

Harry furrowed his brow. "This? You mean showering with someone?"

"No, we did that all the time. I mean being naked with a man. Having your hands on me. I'm not used to that."

"It's making you uncomfortable."

Red couldn't help glancing down at the bulge in his briefs which seemed to be straining to get closer to the big man in front of him. 'Uncomfortable' wasn't the word he'd use. Horny more like. He saw Harry follow his gaze down and blushed—again.

"Don't feel embarrassed about being aroused. This is normal, especially at your age," Harry said. "Most guys pop boners at awkward moments."

Red swore his cheeks were on fire. "I've never been with anyone before."

"Are you gay?"

"I am," Red finally admitted and it felt like a relief to say it out loud. "But I was never going to let a Greencoat know. I didn't want to be chosen. I didn't know about the alternative." He clamped down on his jaw, not wanting to break down again. He was sick of crying.

He expected Harry to tug him into his arms again. Red had spent a lot of time in Harry's arms when he was upset. It suddenly occurred to him, none of the other brothers or boys had held him, not even Lyle.

But Harry just took Red's hands in his. "I know we keep saying this, but you don't have to do anything you don't want to, Red, and that includes being in a shower with me. I offered as you were exhausted and distressed, but it doesn't come with an expectation of anything more. I'll take care of you only if you want me to."

"Your brothers, they all chose boys." Red saw the moment Harry understood what he was trying to say, as his eyes widened and he took a step back, dropping Red's hands. He looked horrified.

"I...no...I can't have this conversation here. Let's get dry and warm." Harry shut off the water and stepped out, wrapping himself in a huge towel and placing one around Red's shoulders. "I'll fetch you something warm to wear, then we'll sit down and talk about this. Do you want Lyle here too? Maybe we ought to discuss this with the family."

"No!" It came out like a yell. Red took a deep breath and tried again. "Just you. I only want to talk with you."

Harry regarded him for a moment, then nodded. "Okay. Stay here."

Once he was gone, Red quickly stripped off his briefs, dried himself, then waited until Harry reappeared.

Harry handed him a pile of clothes he must have taken straight off the dresser in his room. "I'm gonna get dressed. When you're ready, come and talk to me."

Red dropped the damp towel with relief and slipped on the briefs, long-sleeved T-shirt, sweatpants, and a hoodie that had seen better days. He hung up the towel, then took the socks to put on in the bedroom, only to stop stock-still at the sight of Harry's naked ass as he bent over to pull up briefs and sweats. The man had freckles on his butt too. Red dragged his gaze away from the sight of the heavy balls between his thighs. His cock twitched again.

"Ah, good, you ready to talk?" Harry smiled at him as he realized Red was behind him. "Come sit on the chair."

For the first time, Red noticed the huge chair next to a table by the window.

Large enough for two men.

"I'll sit here," Harry said, and made himself comfortable on the end of the bed.

He smiled at Red and waited for him to sit in the chair. Red held back his smile. Harry looked kind of ridiculous perched on the end of the bed while Red was swallowed up by the chair.

But Harry seemed determined to continue their conversation. "Now, let's talk about what you said in the bathroom."

"I didn't mean to make you angry," Red said.

"You didn't," Harry assured him. "But I've got to say, it's clarified something Lyle mentioned. He said you thought of us as Greencoats."

Red decided Lyle was too perceptive for his own good. "I don't think you're the same, but..."

"But?"

Red didn't see any anger in Harry's expression, so he decided to tell the truth. "You won't let me leave here. Your brothers have boys they've chosen. They punish the boys. They do," he insisted as Harry narrowed his eyes. "I heard Vinny talk about it. What's the difference between you and a Greencoat?"

HARRY

"Love, Red. That's the difference."

Red shook his head. "They told us they loved us too. And the way they treated us was for our own good."

Harry wasn't sure whether to cry or vomit, but it wasn't anything he hadn't heard before. He leaned forward and squeezed Red's hand.

"That's not love. It's coercion. The boys here, Lyle, Vinny, Aaron, Jack, and even Matt, are here because they want to be. They were all given the option to leave. Matt does, although he always comes back. Damien tried to push Vinny out but that boy wasn't having any of it. Aaron left, but he came back too. What I'm saying is, they had choices."

Red clenched his fists. "Then why are you keeping me here?"

"Because we don't know how old you are. The second we know you're eighteen, we'll give you money to start your new life and we'll drive you down to town to get the bus."

"I don't believe you."

"I won't lie to you, Red. I'll drive you down myself. It's a promise."

The moment he said it, Harry hated the idea, but the look of relief on Red's face told him he'd said the right thing. He remembered how Damien had felt, sure he had to give Vinny a chance to venture out into the world after years of being locked up, even though it killed him to let Vinny go. Well, now Harry was feeling that. He wasn't in love with Red, but he had feelings for the boy.

"What difference does it make if they can't find out who I am?" Red asked. "I could pick a birthday."

Harry pressed his lips together. "Alec and Jake should be having this conversation with you, not me."

"Yeah, but you're the one here. So spill."

"You need a social security number to get a job, driver's license, accommodation, or to go to college. No birth certificate, no social security number. You're effectively an illegal immigrant. It could take years to get you papers and, in the meantime, you're stuck here."

Red stared at him, his mouth open. "No! Years? I can't stay on this mountain for years."

Harry was sure Red hadn't thought any of this through. Why would he, when he had no idea how the outside world worked? Harry needed to talk to Aaron fast. Jake's boy had gotten fake papers when he ran away from home. Harry didn't want Red to do that.

"Red, take a deep breath. This is not a prison. It's home, your home. You can stay here as our foster, and under eighteen as far as everyone is concerned until Alec and Jake prove otherwise. It's your best option until you have papers. It's not a bad life and we could help you to prepare for the outside world. You know Gruff would love another student."

Harry saw the panic building in Red's expression, the shallow breaths in his chest, beads of sweat on his forehead, and his fists clenching. He stood, picked Red up, and sat on the seat, snuggling them together, not caring about Red's wet hair soaking into his clothes. Red clutched onto Harry, his fingers curling around Harry's hoodie.

"Take deep breaths and relax," Harry rumbled, holding him close.

"I'm so tired," Red murmured.

"I know."

"I've got no control over anything."

Harry didn't point out he had no control over anything before. That was a world Red had known his entire life. "Just let Alec and Jake do their job. That's what they're good at."

Red nodded slowly. "I'll stay until they find out who I am. But you better keep your promise."

"I'll always keep my promise, boy."

Harry rocked Red and, after a while, Red's breathing deepened, and he fell asleep, blowing small puffs of air against Harry's chest. He wondered whether to tuck Red into his bed or let him sleep here for a while. The boy was small enough that his weight wasn't an issue. Harry yawned and leaned back in the seat to make himself more comfortable. Red grumbled, but when Harry hushed him, he settled down again.

Harry must have dozed, because he woke at the sound of a knock.

"Yeah," he mumbled.

The door opened and Gruff put his head around. "Hey." He lowered his voice when he saw Red was asleep. "Lyle was worried when you didn't come back down."

"He needed a shower, then we talked. I think he's finally understood the situation."

Gruff grinned at him. "Then he fell asleep on you."

"He was wiped. We both are," Harry admitted, yawning.

"I'll leave you to sleep if you want."

"I need coffee. I'm gonna hafta deal with the horses before nightfall."

"PJ and I have done that already. I can bring you up coffee. You stay with your boy."

"Thanks, little brother. He's not my boy."

Gruff rolled his eyes and pointed to Red. "Sure he's not. I'll be back in a minute."

Harry flipped him off and Gruff chuckled.

"Hey, Gruff. Could Red become your student too?"

Gruff's face lit up. "I'd love another student. Some of the local fosters are talking about joining us too because they're struggling in the schools."

"We could end up with a Kingdom Mountain school."

"I don't know about that. I'm not trained. We'll start small. These guys deserve a safe space to learn to read and write."

Harry smiled at his brother. He was finally getting to do the one thing he'd always wanted, become a teacher.

"Maybe we can find you some online teaching courses."

Gruff went pink. "I've already started," he admitted. "I want to do the best for our boys."

"They're lucky to have you," Harry said.

"And Red is lucky to have you." Gruff pointedly looked at the sleeping boy.

"He needed a shoulder."

"And a lap?"

"Maybe that too," Harry agreed, holding Red a little tighter.

Red wasn't the first boy who'd cried sitting in Harry's lap. But maybe the first one who had nothing to call his own, not even his name.

"Coffee?" he asked hopefully.

Gruff rolled his eyes. "Yeah, yeah, and Harry?"

"Yeah?"

"Thanks. For thinking I could help these boys."

Harry smiled. "I don't think, Gruff. I know."

So maybe Harry noticed Gruff's eyes gleaming suspiciously bright as he left Harry's bedroom. But Harry had watched his little brother develop into a kind and loving Daddy, and now a patient teacher.

"I'm so lucky to have my family," Harry whispered into Red's damp, bright hair.

Red made a noise which could have been agreement and settled back down to sleep. He wasn't ready to wake any time soon.

Harry closed his eyes and dozed again until he heard the door open. He blinked owlishly at Jack coming in with two cups. "Hey, I didn't expect to see you earlier. I thought you were gone for the day."

"PJ missed me," Jack said. "Coffee for you and chocolate in the travel cup for Red when he wakes up."

"You mean he rang you constantly until you returned?"

PJ and Jack were still new enough to be in the honeymoon phase. Or as Damien put it, for PJ to be a possessive pain in the ass.

"Something like that," Jack agreed, grinning at Harry. "It was okay. Aaron and I were on our way back. PJ wants to know if you want us to get the supplies for the barn. He's got to go into town."

"Thanks, but I'll go tomorrow. I want to take Red to the diner."

"You know how to show a boy a good time," Jack teased. "Here, take the coffee before it gets cold and Lyle shouts at me." He put the travel mug on the small table by the window.

Harry took a long slurp of the hot coffee and sighed. "I needed this."

"I'll talk to Red when he's ready," Jack said. "I know he's struggling. I could take him out for the day...if PJ agrees."

"Thanks," Harry said gratefully. He'd sit on PJ if he had to. "I think he'll appreciate it."

Then once again, Harry was alone with his thoughts. He sipped his coffee, wondering how the hell they were going to find birth details for a boy who didn't exist.

Red sat up, yawning, and scratching his belly. "Did I fall asleep?"

"For about an hour."

"Were you talking to someone?"

"Gruff, then Jack."

"It sounded like rumbling beneath my ear." Red smacked his mouth a couple of times. "I need a drink."

Harry leaned over to get the travel mug and handed it to Red. "Your wish is my command."

Red raised one eyebrow. "You want *me* to command *you*?"

"Isn't gonna happen. I'm the one who gives the orders around here."

"Oh yeah?" Red said. "You sure about that?"

Harry gave him a steady look. "Are you challenging me, boy?"

8

RED

Red had been joking. Well, teasing really. But from the look on Harry's face, he didn't find Red's challenge funny. He was deadly serious. It was as if the laidback bear had suddenly snapped into a different man. Someone dominant...a Daddy. Red felt his heart pound faster at the thought. Could he obey when Harry snapped his fingers? Just like that?

He was sitting on the man's lap, and he wondered if he could obey him! Red needed a reality check.

"Hey," Harry murmured.

Red looked at Harry. "I didn't mean to anger you."

Harry's smile was gentle. "You didn't, but there are boundaries you can't cross, not even as a friend."

Distressed, but not sure whether it was because he'd made a friend angry, or it had unsettled him, Red chewed on his bottom lip.

Harry tugged it free. "Drink your chocolate."

Red decided to blame his feelings on being discombobulated at waking up on Harry's lap. He remembered Harry picking him up and curling into his body. It was so comfortable and soothing. But he was still there and had no desire to move, even though Harry had given him a mild scolding.

Harry seemed to be lost in thought and Red waited for a few minutes, but as he didn't speak, he said, "I'm sorry we didn't get a chance to get your supplies."

"No problem. We'll go tomorrow. We can take care of the horses first thing and then drive into town."

"Okay."

Red yawned, swallowing the word, pleased when Harry encouraged him to snuggle into his chest again. He knew they'd have to move soon enough, but Harry's body was comfortable and warm, so he did as he was told. It was too easy just to obey the big bear, Red thought wryly. It was something he would have to get over when he left.

Harry ran a soothing hand down Red's back. "Are you hungry?"

"A little," Red admitted. "I haven't eaten today."

"And then you were sick. We'll go downstairs and see if PJ's left anything for us."

Red had quickly learned Harry's brother had a reputation for eating everything in the refrigerator unless he was specifically told not to. Lyle labeled covered dishes with warnings for PJ to leave them alone. But Red figured the enormous man was responsible for most of the physical labor on the farm. No wonder he was hungry all the time.

"Do we need to take care of the horses now?"

"Gruff and PJ have done that already so I could focus on you. And before I forget, Jack has offered to take you out. He says he knows it can be overwhelming here."

Red felt the back of his eyes prickle. He wasn't used to

people doing things for each other out of kindness. He swallowed hard and tackled the thing playing on his mind.

"I was rude to your family."

"Yes, you were." Harry sighed. "I know you're scared and frustrated, but my brothers and their boys don't deserve your anger. They're good people, Red."

"I'll apologize to them."

"Even Vinny?" There was a hint of humor in Harry's voice.

"Even Vinny," Red muttered.

Harry chuckled ruefully. "He can be scarily possessive over his Daddy."

"You can say that again." Red sucked in a breath. "How will you punish me?"

"I'm not going to punish you, Red. You were rude, but you realize it. An apology is all that's needed."

Red was confused. "But I deserve to be punished. The Greencoats would beat me for the way I spoke to you."

"We're not Greencoats," Harry said gently.

"But you punish your boys."

"That's between a Daddy and his boy. I can promise you each boy knows he's loved and forgiven." Harry patted his back. "Maybe you can find a way of helping Vinny. How are you at peeling potatoes?"

"I've never done it before. I never worked in the kitchens."

"I forgot that. It's tedious," Harry admitted, "but we eat a lot of potatoes. Vinny's always glad of the assistance. Offer to help him and ask him to show you."

"You think that'll make him like me?" If he was stuck here, he needed to make friends with the boys, or at least be able to live with them.

"You can't make anyone like you, Red, but you can show them you can be a friend."

"I've never had a real friend," Red admitted. "Just boys I shared a dorm with."

Harry sighed underneath him. "Just get to know us. We're all different."

Red thought about it. Maybe it was time he stopped being so angry at everyone. It wasn't their fault that his records were lost. "What can I do for Lyle?"

"I don't know. Why don't you ask him? Damien would probably appreciate a hand with the accounts."

"I can do that." Accounts were the one thing he could do.

Harry's belly rumbled loudly beneath him, and he couldn't help chuckling.

"Let's go eat," Harry suggested, "and feed the beast."

That sounded like a great idea but first Red had something to do.

"I need the bathroom," he admitted.

Harry put him on his feet, and he hurried into the bathroom, still amazed at how strong Harry was. He'd picked him up like he weighed nothing. Red blushed at what a turn-on it was.

He stared at himself in the mirror. Despite what he said to anyone else, he was in danger of having feelings for Harry.

"It's just because he's been kind to you. It doesn't mean anything. He doesn't want a boy and you don't want a Daddy."

Red splashed his face with water and attempted to calm the tousled mess of his hair. It didn't look any better and he gave up.

Harry was waiting for him by the open door when he returned to the bedroom.

"Could I get my hair cut in town tomorrow?"

"Brad can do that for you," Harry said. "He does everyone's." Red squinted at him because Harry needed a haircut, and he laughed. "He kinda has to wrestle us to get it done. But seriously, he's good. He was taught by one of the barbers." His laughter faded. "Not everyone will take our custom. We've found it easier to do as much as we can for ourselves."

"Because you're gay?"

Harry shrugged. "Seven gay brothers. It's too much for some people to handle. It's a small town. And most folks are fine. We know where we're welcome and where we avoid."

"Do they fight you?" Red asked harshly.

Now it was Harry's turn to squint. "Have you seen us? No one picks a fight unless they're liquored up. No, they just give us the cold shoulder."

Red nodded his head, irrationally angry at the thought of small-minded people being rude to Harry. Then he felt ashamed. Hadn't he been the same to the family?

Harry wrapped an arm around his shoulders. "Come on, let's eat, before I find you tasty." He chuckled at Red's squeak. "Don't worry, cannibalism isn't one of my kinks."

"I should hope not." But Red didn't move away from him.

To his surprise, the kitchen was empty. Harry picked up a note left on the table. "Brad's out and won't be back until tomorrow. Alec is out with Matt. The others are having a play date in town and will be back later."

"What does that mean?"

"Daddy and boy time. It means we've got the house to ourselves and—" Harry's eyes lit up. "Lyle has left us a pie for dinner." He went over to look in the refrigerator and pulled out a large pie dish. "That boy is an angel."

For the first time, Red's mouth watered at the thought of food. Up to now, it had been a real struggle to eat anything beyond the smallest portions. From talking with Lyle, that wasn't unusual for a Kingdom boy. When you grew up on one meal a day, having the luxury of eating three large meals was overwhelming. It would be a long time before he could think of food and not feel sick, but right now he was hungry.

"You can help me prepare dinner," Harry suggested.

Red stared at him uncertainly. "We're not eating the pie?"

"We're eating the pie with potatoes and vegetables. When you go out into the world on your own, you'll need to know how to cook."

Harry was right, but somehow the thought had never occurred to him. He'd never had to prepare food for himself. Even here, Lyle or Vinny did the cooking. That was going to have to change.

Suck it up, Red, he told himself firmly. *If you're gonna survive away from here, learn everything, including peeling potatoes.*

Internal lecture over, he gave Harry a nod. "What do I have to do?"

Harry beamed at him. "Good boy."

Red jolted at the 'boy'. It didn't mean anything. The brothers called all the boys that. So why did his heart just give an unexpected leap?

"Red?"

"Yeah? Sorry."

"Is everything okay?"

Red saw Harry's concerned expression. "It's fine. I'm just worried about poisoning you."

Harry gave his booming laugh and rubbed his belly. "You won't do that. I've got a cast-iron stomach. Before Lyle came into our lives, we needed it. Right, potatoes!"

An hour later, Red stared at the remains of the dinner on the table. There wasn't a lot left of the pie. They'd both been starving. "It took an hour to cook and ten minutes to eat?"

"It's always the way," Harry assured him. "But it's worth it. How do you feel? You ate a Brenner-size dinner."

"I'm not sure if I can move," Red confessed, looking down at his decidedly rounded belly.

"We'll make a Brenner of you yet."

"I don't think I'm built to be a bear."

"We were all your size once," Harry said.

"Uh-huh. When was that?"

Harry had to think about it for a moment. "Twelve, maybe thirteen."

"I'm older than that," Red said. "Like I said, I don't think I'm destined to be a bear. But that was the best dinner I ever had."

"And you helped cook it."

"I don't think I like peeling potatoes. Why does Vinny do it?"

"Therapy sessions," Harry said.

Red blinked at the cryptic comment. "Huh?"

"I'll let him explain. Let's clear everything away."

"We have to tidy up too?" Red said, before he could think.

"Yup," Harry said cheerfully. "Come on, Cinderfella. Let's whistle while we work. No wait, I've gotten my fairy-tales mixed up."

"Cinder-what? You want me to whistle? Seriously?"

Harry shook his head. "Oh boy. I can see I've got a lot to explain. What do you know about fairy tales?"

Red wrinkled his forehead. "Fairy what?"

"Where is Gruff when I need him," Harry muttered. "He's the teacher, not me."

"I need you," Red said, surprising them both, and seeing the sudden smile from Harry, it was worth it.

HARRY

It was rare for everyone to be out at the same time. It unsettled Harry, but he tried not to let Red see it, because he could see how much Red relaxed when he didn't have to face the family. It was as if he drew breath for the first time. Harry had to admit he couldn't understand it. How could someone who had grown up around people all the time, struggle so much with his loving family?

"Let's clear up and I'll explain what a fairytale is."

As they loaded the dishwasher, Harry thought about what to say, because there were the *Grimm* kind of fairytales and the *Disney* kind and let's face it, they weren't on the same plane. Harry had always preferred the happy versions. Since discovering the fate of the Kingdom children, Harry thought it was too much like the unhappy tales.

"Harry?" Red interrupted his musing. "You were going to tell me about fairytales."

Harry hummed. "Wait a minute. Finish drying the dishes and sit down at the table."

He legged it up to his bedroom and grabbed his little used tablet. He brought it downstairs and after a few minutes of remembering how to use the tablet, he went through an explanation of how fairy tales originated and the different kinds of stories.

He grinned at Red. "We have a running joke in the family that Gruff, Damien, and PJ all found their boys with a fairytale ending. The Disney kind, not Grimm." But Red didn't return his smile. "Red? What's wrong."

Red furrowed his brow. "So it's just made up. A story. It's not real."

"No, it's not real. It's fiction. But fairy tales are stories of hope, courage, and dreams coming true."

At least the kind he preferred. The ones where the good guys didn't die.

"Dreams are for kids," Red said bluntly. "And not kids where I grew up. We knew that the only dreams we had were nightmares, and life ended as soon as we were eighteen."

Harry's heart clenched at Red's heart-breaking tale, and then he processed what Red had said. "You knew the disappeared had died."

"I knew something had happened to them. I'm not stupid. I didn't know they were eaten by alligators."

Harry heard the heartache in his shaky voice. He pulled Red into his arms. "Those men, the CEO, and the Green-coats, they will pay for what they did to all the boys."

"It won't bring them back." Red's voice was muffled against Harry's hoodie. "They won't get their happy ever after, Harry. They didn't get a fairy tale ending. They died horribly."

Harry held him tighter. "No, they won't. But saving Lyle has changed the ending for so many boys, I promise you. I know you don't want to believe it but it's true."

Red raised his head. "Even for a boy like me?"

"Especially," Harry growled, "for a boy like you."

He couldn't help himself. He bent and brushed Red's mouth, pressing the lightest of kisses on his lush lips. Red shivered against him, and Harry came to his senses.

"I'm sorry. That was wrong of me."

Red's eyes were so wide, it was almost comical. "No, it wasn't. I wanted you to kiss me."

Harry sighed and disentangled himself from Red, cursing himself for being so weak, and cursing himself even more for putting the hurt look in his sweet boy's eyes. He enfolded Red's hands in his, not willing to let him go completely.

"Look, we don't know how you came to be at the water park, but we do know how it always ends for the boys."

Red pressed his lips together. "No happy ending for them."

"I want to give you the happy ending, my boy. I really do. But there are laws and I have to obey them. I'm a lot older than you—"

"I don't care about the age gap," Red burst out. "None of your brothers care."

Harry expelled a long breath. "They do care, I can promise you that. All the boys were eighteen before my brothers claimed them, including Vinny, no matter how hard he pushed."

"So you expect us to wait until we find out my date of birth? That could take years." Red sounded horrified.

"Then we'll wait as long as it takes." Harry fixed Red with a piercing stare. He had to make his boy understand. "Tell me who you'd trust more, the man who waited to make sure everything was legal or the man who took his pleasure without thinking of what was right for his boy?"

Red tugged his hands away and Harry let him go, even though he didn't want to. "But I'm not going to be here forever. I want to know what it's like in the outside world."

Well, at least Harry knew now, and really, wasn't that what he'd said from the beginning? He didn't want a boy. Red didn't want a Daddy. He'd just been here to take care of Red as he coped with yet another foster home.

So why did his heart ache so much at the thought of losing Red? He forced a smile on his face. "I'll help you find your place in the outside world. I promise. You'll have a home, a job, and be safe." Harry ran a finger along Red's jaw, feeling the lightest of stubble under his fingertips. Red was old enough to need to shave. "Being a Daddy is about more than sex. It's about nurturing too and that means knowing what's best for you, even when you don't know it yourself."

Red scowled at him. "I can decide what's best for me."

"You didn't answer my question. Who do you trust more? The man who waits to know it's legal or the one who takes his pleasure regardless?"

"That's unfair," Red whispered.

"On both of us," Harry agreed. "But it's what men like me do."

Red huffed as he subsided in the seat. "What if I find myself another man? One who doesn't care so much?"

"I'll kill him," Harry assured him and watched Red's eyes go comically wide. "I mean it. I'll kill any man who doesn't treat you with the proper respect. And if I didn't, any one of my brothers would throw him off the mountain, then throw me after him for not having your back. You are under our care and that means protecting you from other men."

Red may have thought he was joking, but they had all taught each other how to respect the men in their care. It was why Red had become Harry's responsibility. Harry had learned a lot from Brad and Damien and then his younger brothers. Even PJ, who was the biggest tease on the planet, had matured into a Daddy to be proud of.

He could see the myriad of emotions in Red's expression. Angry, yes. Red was annoyed that Harry had pushed him away. He wanted Harry as much as Harry wanted him. But he was a teenager and horny. Harry could see the relief too, and following Harry's explanation, maybe a bit of respect. Red didn't know what to think.

"Before I go, will you..." Red licked his lips. "Will you take me to bed?"

"If it's legal." And if Harry was still at the farm. Hell, he would come back to show Red what it was like to have a man who cared enough to make love to him before he found his way in the world.

And if he did it right, no one would ever match up to him. Harry was sure of that.

9

Red jumped at the thunderous knock on the door. He'd been deep in a dream where Harry was kissing him and telling him he loved him and begging him not to leave.

"Red, Harry says move your butt," PJ bellowed. "You've got ten minutes before he leaves for town."

What on earth? Red sat upright in bed. "Okay," he rasped out. He swallowed and tried again. "I'll be downstairs in five minutes."

"'Kay, I'll tell him. Don't go back to sleep."

"That's what *you* do," Jack grumbled.

Red heard them bicker at each other as they went downstairs. He jumped into the clothes he'd laid out on the dresser the night before and ran into the bathroom to wash his face and brush his teeth. Red grimaced at himself in the mirror. His hair looked wilder than normal, no matter how hard he tried to flatten it.

"I'm going off the mountain," he said to his reflection.

Just the thought of it made his heart pound. Harry had kept his promise.

That made Red think of the other promise Harry had made to him the previous night. They'd gone to bed after that—separate bedrooms, because as Harry said, he couldn't trust himself not to sleep in the same bed as Red and not want to hold him so tight.

Red had opened his mouth to point out he wouldn't mind, but Harry had shaken his head and pointed to the stairs.

"Don't tempt me, boy. My willpower ain't that strong."

Red smiled as he ran up the stairs. Harry was just as horny as him. Red held that to himself, sure now that Harry would keep his promise. Had Harry come in and whispered that he loved him? Or maybe he just dreamed that. It was hard to pick out what was real and what was a dream.

But now there was something else fun to do.

"Red!" Harry bellowed.

Shit! Red was too busy going all gooey about what might happen and not focusing on the day ahead.

He ran down the stairs to join Harry. "I'm sorry. I must have overslept."

"It's okay. I should have woken you earlier." Harry grimaced. "There was a family discussion, and it got a little heated."

Red felt his stomach clench. "About me?"

To his relief, Harry shook his head. "No, kid. You're fine. I...uh...told them my plans and..." He took a deep breath. "Let's just say Damien didn't take it too well."

From the tightness around his eyes and pinched face, Harry was more upset than he was admitting.

Red laid a hand on his arm. "I'm sorry. Do you wanna talk about it?"

Harry placed his hand over Red's. "Maybe over break-fast, yeah? It'd be good to talk to you."

Red glowed as he dressed in his jacket and boots. Harry trusted him enough to talk to him about something impor-tant. That was unexpected. He also noticed how quiet the cabin was.

"Where is everybody?"

"The boys took themselves off to the playroom. My brothers are anywhere but near me," Harry admitted. "It got loud. I'm surprised it didn't wake you up."

"I didn't hear a thing," Red said, flushing as he remem-bered what he'd been dreaming about. "Will you guys be okay?"

"We always get over it, kid," Damien said, emerging from the kitchen. He looked worse than Harry if that were possible. "Eventually."

The tension between Damien and Harry could be cut with a knife. Red looked between the two huge men. God, he could feel the ache in their hearts.

"Whatever it is, I know you two will sort it. Because that's what you do as brothers." They squinted at him, and he flushed. "Look, you're all as annoying as hell to outsiders like me, but I'm envious of the love between you guys. You'd go through fire for each other." Harry and Damien were both nodding. "Then talk it out later, whatever it is. But hug now. Because you both hurt like hell and I can feel it here." Red placed a hand over his heart.

No hesitation. They were in each other's arms and Red swore at least one of them sobbed. He saw Vinny lurking in the doorway, Rexy at his feet, his lips pressed together. They exchanged worried glances and looked away. This wasn't anything to do with them. It was between the brothers. Then Harry and Damien stepped back, wiped their eyes and if they looked a little bloodshot Red didn't mention it.

"Let's get breakfast," Harry said to Red.

It wasn't resolved, whatever it was, but they were family, and they would handle it.

Red pushed it to one side as he climbed into Harry's rust bucket of a Chevy. He'd almost forgotten he drove it the first evening he arrived. "You take such good care of the horses, yet you drive this."

Harry snorted. "I'd never drive if I didn't have to. I love riding. But I'm not riding down that road. It's quieter now Kingdom Mountain Park is gone. The drivers coming up here were a nightmare. But we still get idiots who think they can drive like maniacs on the road. I wouldn't risk our horses." He started the engine and turned to Red. "If you get scared just close your eyes. I've been driving the road all my life. You're safe with me."

Red hoped so, because he didn't want to admit he was terrified already, and they hadn't moved yet.

Harry patted his leg. "I've got you."

"You'd better," Red muttered.

Red tried not to whimper down the mountain road. He closed his eyes but not being able to see was even scarier. Harry took Red's hand and placed it on his solid thigh.

"Hold onto me. I can't hold your hand. I need it to drive. So hold onto my leg."

Red did as he was told and found the solid warmth helped, as did the stories Harry told him about his brothers and growing up on the Christmas tree farm. By the time they reached the lumber yard, Red had almost relaxed.

It didn't take long for Harry to deal with the supplies. Red hung about in the background. He was aware of the curious gazes on him but when Harry said, "Red's a

Kingdom foster boy," the curiosity turned to pity. Red wasn't sure which he hated the most.

Then they were back in the Chevy and on their way to the diner.

"We always eat here," Harry confided. "PJ met Jack here. He knocked him unconscious."

Red barked out a laugh. "You know, I could make some remark about that."

Harry flashed him a wry smile. "You'd probably be right, but it was an accident. Jack was standing behind him and got in the way of PJ's arm. It was lucky for Jack, though, as he'd run out of money. PJ offered him somewhere to stay and Jack never left."

Red wanted to make a caustic remark, but he knew Harry wouldn't appreciate him being disrespectful about his family again, and he also knew PJ and Jack were very happy together. PJ treated Jack as if he were something precious, and Jack ignored PJ's crassness because the huge man offered him love and security, something he'd never had.

The town wasn't much, but Red stared out, fascinated. The diner was on the outskirts of town and when Harry guided him in, Red saw it was busy, every table and booth full of people talking and eating. The volume of chatter hit him like a wall. It was almost overwhelming and if Harry hadn't been behind him, he would have bolted.

A waitress approached them with a smile. "Harry, it's been a while. Is this your boy?"

Red turned a pleading look on Harry who flashed him an apologetic grin.

Harry bent and kissed her on the cheek. "Hi Sheila, this is Red, our Kingdom foster boy. He helps me with the horses."

Sheila gave Red a bright smile. "Right, hi, Red, welcome. Take the booth at the back."

Wrapping his arm around Red's shoulders, Harry led him to the booth. They slid in and Red glanced around, not hiding his curiosity.

"I've never eaten anywhere like this," Red admitted.

"Nor had Lyle and Vinny. They love coming here. They can't go to the bar yet, so Gruff and Damien bring them here as a treat."

"Do your brothers go to the bar without them?"

Red had heard a lot about the bar from Aaron and Jack who'd both worked there. He suspected, although no one would outright admit it, that there was something suspect about Aaron's age. Red could count and Aaron kept talking about Rapunzel years. Something didn't add up.

Harry shook his head. "Gruff and Damien would rather be with their boys than apart from them. I miss the days when we all visited the bar," he confessed. "Now it's just me and Brad, and occasionally Alec if Matt's not around. Jake's not there to start a fight."

Red regarded him for a moment. "It's been a complete change in your lives, hasn't it?"

"It turned our world upside down. Sheila, is that coffee pot for me?"

"Would I leave you without coffee?" she teased as she filled the cup in front of him. "Red, hot chocolate is on its way."

Red's mouth dropped open. "How—"

"PJ," she said. "He and Jack were in here yesterday. Usual, Harry?"

Harry beamed at her. "Thanks, Sheila." He turned to Red when she left. "I'm sorry, do you want something else to drink?"

Red huffed out a laugh. "No, this is fine. What's the usual? Oatmeal?"

"Steak and eggs. You'll get the same. Just eat what you can, and I'll finish off the rest."

"She didn't ask me what I wanted."

"Well, no, she wouldn't." Harry sounded like it was a done deal.

Red shook his head. He didn't understand this world, but maybe he wasn't meant to.

HARRY

Red dozed most of the journey up the mountain road. Harry let him sleep and enjoyed the drive, with a full belly and a sleepy boy next to him.

As Harry parked the Chevy in its usual spot, Red raised his head and blinked sleepily as he tried to focus. "Hey, I'm sorry, did I sleep all the way?"

"It's fine," Harry assured him. "It was nice you could relax enough to sleep."

Red smiled almost shyly at him. "Thanks for taking me out today."

"You're welcome. I like getting away from here too."

"But not for long," Red teased.

"Not for long," Harry agreed, then thought about the fight around the kitchen table that morning. How would the family cope if he left? How would *he* cope if he struggled when his brothers were away for a day?

He expelled a breath. "Come on, let's go annoy my brothers."

He was sure Red muttered a "Hallelujah," under his breath but he didn't repeat it. Harry grinned. Red was one

boy who was always going to be a square peg in the
Brenner family circle. Just like Matt really.

Harry pushed Red ahead of him into the kitchen, only
for Red to come to a halt. "What's wrong, kid?" Then he
saw who was at the table. "Hey, Alec, you're back."

Alec's smile was tight, and Harry felt his heart squeeze.
"What's wrong?" he demanded.

Ignoring him, Alec stood, walked over, and held an
envelope out to Red. "We have the information I think
you're gonna want to look at."

Instead of taking it, Red looked at Harry who reached
around him, took the envelope from Alec, and handed it
to Red.

"I think you should open it," Harry said, his voice
gentle, trying not to spook him.

Red opened the envelope with shaking fingers and
pulled out a piece of paper. Harry stood by him, a hand on
Red's back, wondering if this was the moment his new-
found happiness ended. His boy, no, Red wasn't Harry's
boy. The *kid* stared at the paper and then looked at Harry,
his blue eyes wide.

"My name is Stephen." He read it again. "I know who I
am now," Red said in wonder. "My name is Stephen
Thompson," he managed faintly.

Harry looked over his shoulder. Stephen Kade Thompson. "You've got your name, kid. Hi, Stephen."

Red gave him a wobbly grin and stared at the birth
certificate again.

"You were given up by your birth mom," Alec said. "She
was very young. We don't know anything more yet."

Harry read over his shoulder. "You'll have to decide if
you're a Stephen or a Steve."

"Give him a chance, bro," PJ said. "He's only been a Stephen for a hot moment."

"I kinda like the name Red. It's the only name I've ever known," Red said, finally.

"You can call yourself what you like, kid," Harry pointed out.

"Less of the kid. Take a look at your date of birth, Red," Jake said.

Red worked it out in his head, then he frowned. "I really am twenty-one."

Harry blinked. Twenty-one? That couldn't be right. No one survived past eighteen. Even Lyle and Vinny looked confused.

"I don't understand." Red looked at Alec and Jake. "How did I survive an extra three years without being disappeared? Where were my records?"

"The CEO had your birth certificate and he'd chosen you as a replacement for his boy," Jake said. "We discovered in his records that he did know how you arrived at the water park. He wanted you as his. I'm sorry, we don't know why it didn't happen when you were eighteen. But they were planning to swap you over within the week. It was only our intervention that saved you both."

"Fuck."

It was like the whole family swore at the same time. There was a rustle of notes and coins in the swear jar but Red just sat there, ignoring everyone. It was as if his brain had taken a ride on the rollercoaster and left him behind.

"Red?" Harry said gently, concerned about him.

Red looked at Harry. "I'm twenty-one."

"Yes."

"I'm twenty-one," Red repeated.

Harry gave him a tight grin. "Twenty-one. I can't believe it."

"I always suspected I was older than everyone said."

Harry studied the boy. He wasn't tall or well-developed, which maybe was the reason they thought he was younger. But from what Gruff told him, he'd always been intellectually ahead of his peers, at least in math. Maybe that's why he'd ended up in the accounts office. The Greencoats had been pleased to find someone who could handle the volume of money the park took every day.

"I don't know what to think," Red admitted.

"At least Harry can take you to the Tin Bar now," PJ suggested and laughed at Harry's sudden growl.

"Not on a Tuesday night," Aaron said. "The Daddies will be all over him." He held his hands up at Harry's scowl. "What? I'm just saying."

"Aaron has a point," Jake agreed, with a lazy smile at his boy.

"Me and Jack could take you and Harry," PJ agreed.

Aaron scowled and PJ shrugged.

"It's not my fault you're too young."

"I worked there," Aaron snapped.

"Underage. Really underage," Jake pointed out. He laughed as Aaron huffed and reeled him in for a hug and a bone-melting kiss.

"I need to take care of the horses," Harry said, standing up abruptly. He couldn't stay here any longer and watch his brother's happiness while his heart broke. Harry couldn't help himself. He'd fallen in love with Red and hadn't realized it until now. How could he have been so blind? He loved everything about Red, from his wit and intelligence to his quick temper and even his snappiness. He wanted nothing more than to protect him, keep him safe, and make sure he was happy.

Red looked up from the table. "I can help."

Harry shook his head. "You stay here. Alec and Jake can help you with what you have to do next." He virtually ran out of the kitchen, leaving Red with his brothers.

"What's up with him?" he heard PJ ask. Then a yelp. "What did you do that for?"

One of the brothers had obviously kicked PJ in the shin.

Harry left the cabin before someone came after him. He didn't want Red to know how unhappy he was. His thoughts kept drifting back to what Aaron had said about the Daddies at the Tin Bar. Harry knew that, if he were to take Red there, there would be a risk of another Daddy laying claim to him. It would kill Harry if Red walked into another Daddy's arms.

Red deserved more than a drink in the bar. His sweet bird deserved to spread his wings and find his true place in the world. But Harry also knew that Red deserved a chance at a better life outside, one that he could call his own. Yes, Harry had fallen in love with Red, but he'd be strong enough to let him go. That's what a good Daddy did, knowing it was time for his boy to move on.

Harry retreated to the barn, cooing to the horses as he entered. He smiled as they answered him with a toss of their heads. At least they were pleased to see him. He spent a few hours caring for them and mucking out stalls. He knew the familiar routine should make him feel settled, yet it only added to his conflict. He wanted to feel the comfort of the familiar tasks but found himself wishing for something new. Frustrated, he kept working, trying to make sense of the feelings within him.

The mares nuzzled him as he worked, as if they understood he was upset. Harry sighed and hugged them, grateful for their unconditional love. He could count on them to always be there for him, no matter what.

Once Red left, it would be time Harry found his own path and stepped out into the world. He could apply to vet school next fall. If Red could be brave, so could he. Harry knew it was time he set off on his journey and made something out of himself.

He didn't look up as someone entered the barn. They weren't his boy's lighter footsteps.

"You're an idiot," Brad said.

"He needs to be free." Harry didn't pretend not to understand.

"He needs his Daddy who's being a coward and hiding in the barn."

"I can't hold him back."

He felt a hand on his shoulder, then Brad turned him around. Harry sighed and leaned into his solid, comfortable brother, smelling the familiar scent of pine and chill air and chemicals. Brad was home as were all his other brothers.

They stayed like that for a few minutes before Brad said, "Just tell him you love him, little brother. That's all he needs to know. You owe him that. What happens next is up to him."

"What if he leaves me?"

"Then you've set your boy free and he knows where you are if he falls."

There was an edge to Brad's voice and Harry looked up.

"Did that happen to you?"

Brad just smiled, patted his shoulder, and walked out of the barn, leaving Harry staring after him. Sometimes his brother was as cryptic as his poetry.

Night had fallen, and Harry's belly was growling before

he returned to the house and found Red sitting at the pine table, alone in the kitchen. When he looked up, Harry saw his distraught expression.

"Where have you been?" Red demanded. "Why did you leave me?"

"I had to take care of the horses," Harry answered. "I didn't mean to upset you. I knew you were busy."

"You left me all day. I needed you."

"I'm sorry," Harry looked away, feeling guilty now. He'd walked out just when Red needed him most.

"You said you loved me," Red said accusingly. "I heard you last night."

Harry nodded, embarrassed that Red had heard his whispered confession. "I do love you. But I can't keep you. You're not my boy."

"What if I don't want to leave? What if I want to be your boy?"

"I don't understand," Harry said, confused. "You insisted you wanted to make your own way in the world once you knew your age. Nothing is keeping you here now."

"Except you."

"I won't keep you in a cage. You need your wings."

Red stood and walked over to Harry. "You can't keep me here against my will. But I don't want to leave. I want to stay. With you," he added pointedly.

Harry stared at Red, stunned. "I never imagined you would want to stay," he said. "I thought you wanted to fly off the mountain."

"What is this flying thing you've got going on?" Red demanded. "I can't fly or walk off this damn mountain without you and I don't want to."

Harry shoved a dollar in the swear jar without taking

his gaze away from Red's indignant expression. But the moment was interrupted by the growl in his belly.

Red rolled his eyes. "Stay there. Lyle left us both food in the fridge. I didn't want to eat without you."

Harry sat back and let Red put it together for them. The boy seemed to want to take care of him and Harry was feeling vulnerable enough to admit he needed it tonight.

They ate in silence, but Red watched his every move, Harry could see that. After dinner, Harry thanked Red, summoned his courage, and told him that he wanted nothing more than for Red to be happy and safe wherever life took him.

"You're an idiot, Harry," Red said bluntly. "What makes you think I want to leave you?"

"You should go live in the city, Red. You're going to do big things. I want you to go and find a new life. If I don't encourage you, who will? You should be able to get a job and start a life for yourself," Harry insisted.

"I don't want to leave if you don't want me to. I don't have to go. I can stay here with you and the horses. We can live here on the Christmas tree farm, or wherever you go to school. We can have the future that you've always wanted," Red said softly, eyes pleading.

"You don't mean that, Red. You should be the one to go to school and get qualifications." Harry was never going to stand in Red's way. "You could start your own business. You could travel the world."

"Harry, I don't want to travel without you. How many times do I have to say this? I love you, you big dumb ox," Red said.

Harry scowled at him. "Enough with the names, boy. You can't love me. You're just saying that because you feel you have to."

Red stood up and walked around the table to stand in front of Harry. He reached down and pulled Harry's hands into his. "I love you. I'm not going to run away to the city. I'm not going to leave you. I've been miserable all afternoon without you, Harry. I'm staying here with you. I love you, and I want to be with you."

Harry felt his body relax and his heart fill with happiness. Red loved him. The boy he had grown to love and care for, loved him back. It was everything that Harry had never wanted and now knew it was what he needed.

"Red, are you sure? I don't want you to regret anything. You don't have to stay here just because of me."

"Yes, I'm sure. I want to stay here with you." Red leaned forward and kissed him. "I love you, Daddy. I want to be your boy."

10

RED

The heated shush and giggles from outside in the hallway told Red they were not alone.

He huffed and rolled his eyes at Harry. "Is this the way it's always going to be?" He'd just declared his love for his Daddy and there they were, the Brenner family, waiting to get involved.

Harry grinned at him. "This is it. You've got to suck it up, kid. There's no such thing as privacy in this house."

Red sucked in a deep breath. That was going to change. "Yeah. We'll talk about that later. But first…"

"Yes?"

Red stood and held out his hand and stared, hoping Harry could see all the want and need in his eyes. "Take me upstairs?"

"About time," Vinny muttered as he walked in. "I'm starving."

"You hush up," Damien said. "Harry waited like a good Daddy should. You don't get to scold him for being good."

Vinny grumbled something but Red ignored them both. His whole focus was on Harry. His Daddy had been very respectful, but now Red wanted Harry to quit holding back.

Please say yes. Please don't say no to me.

But Harry seemed to be waiting for something. Red didn't know what. Then, out of the corner of his eye, he caught Vinny mouthing *"Please Daddy,"* at him.

Red gave a small nod and looked at Harry again. "Take me upstairs, please, Daddy?"

Harry let out a breath. He stood and took Red's hand. "We're gonna be busy. Damien?"

Damien rolled his eyes. "Yeah, yeah, we'll do the horses."

Red mouthed *thanks* to Vinny, then he yelped as he was swept off his feet into Harry's arms.

"You take care of him, little brother." Damien patted Harry's shoulder. "Your boy deserves to be looked after."

Suddenly embarrassed, Red buried his face in Harry's neck, feeling his beard tickle him.

"I'll always take care of him," Harry promised.

Red shuddered and Harry held him tighter as he carried him out of the room.

"You're my boy," Harry whispered in his ear.

"You'd better not say no again," Red growled at Harry because he had waited long enough to find the man of his dreams.

Harry raised one copper eyebrow and Red knew he was in trouble.

"We're gonna have a long discussion about the way you talk to everyone, especially me, but later. First, I'm going to take care of my boy."

Red shivered and he wasn't sure if it was the thought of

Harry disciplining him or taking care of him that made him shiver the most. What would Harry do to him?

Harry nudged open the door of his bedroom with his foot. "You're gonna be sleeping in here now."

"We don't—"

"We do," Harry insisted. "You're my boy and you sleep in my arms every night."

Red blinked back the tears that threatened to spill over. His Daddy was so kind to him.

"I'll take care of you, Red, I promise. I know you find it hard to trust people, but you can trust me."

Harry placed Red on his feet. "I'm going to undress you," he whispered.

At Red's nervous nod, he gently undressed them both until they were standing naked together. They stood facing each other in the darkness. The only light was from the moonlight which bathed their skin and tamed their flaming hair.

Red sighed as he smoothed the red fur over Harry's chest, brushing his copper nipples.

Harry shuddered but he pushed Red's hands away. "I want to touch you."

Then his hands moved down Red's arms, his fingertips tracing a line from shoulder to elbow. He continued his journey to Red's wrists, cradling them in his hands before trailing back on the same path. It was soothing, yet tingling at the same time. All Red's senses kicked in. He could smell the scent he had come to associate with Harry beneath the ever-present aromas of pine and horses. He felt like he was the one touching Harry rather than the other way around. Red leaned into him further, his body molding against his in the darkness.

Harry's hands moved to Red's waist, his fingers tracing

the delicate skin of his sides. He moved lower, his hands now cupping Red's hips. Red's breathing increased, his heart beating faster with anticipation.

Harry leaned in, his lips meeting Red's neck in a gentle kiss. His hand moved up Red's spine, his fingertips stroking the sensitive skin of his neck and back. Red gasped, a wave of pleasure radiating through his body.

They stayed like that for some time, motionless and suspended in the moment. Red's body was alive with Harry's touch, his mind and heart completely focused on him.

Red felt complete in Harry's embrace, his body and soul melting together as one. He never wanted it to end, so he stayed there in the moonlight, content to be surrounded by Harry's warmth.

His thoughts were interrupted when Harry began to move, his kisses now traveling further down Red's body. His lips were soft and gentle, leaving a trail of heat in their wake. Red closed his eyes, savoring every sensation that coursed through his veins. He couldn't believe his Daddy could be so gentle.

He hadn't realized he'd said it out loud until Harry said, "This is your first time. I want to take care of you."

Harry continued exploring Red's body with increasing intensity, until he paused at Red's navel, dipping in to taste, moved back up again, and kissed Red on the lips as if he was sealing a promise. A promise that he would take care of him and make him feel loved and cherished forever.

Red made a noise of protest. He wanted to feel of his Daddy's mouth around his cock as he never had before.

Harry leaned forward and kissed him. "Soon, my boy, I promise."

His kisses were sweet and kind, but with the hint of

fiery passion he promised for later. Red hoped his Daddy didn't take too long, because he was so hard, one puff of wind and he might come.

Harry opened his nightstand drawer and pulled out lube and condoms.

"Do we need condoms? I haven't—"

"But I have. We get tested first." Harry pressed a kiss on Red's mouth. "I would never put you at risk, Red."

"Okay," Red said hoarsely, realizing it wasn't up for discussion. He could wait because his Daddy asked him to.

"You might find it easier on your hands and knees," Harry suggested, nudging them to the bed.

Red shook his head. "I need to see you."

I need to know you're not gonna hurt me. But that was something he couldn't say out loud. He didn't want to hurt Harry's feelings.

But his Daddy seemed to understand because he gently slid a pillow under Red's hips. "You just look into my eyes, okay, sweet boy? Don't look away from me."

Even in the darkness, his expression was so open and clear, at that moment all of Red's worries melted away, replaced by the purest happiness he had ever known. The only true happiness he'd ever known, he admitted to himself. He opened himself up to the love between them, letting a lifetime of carefully constructed barriers fall away until nothing was left but Red, naked and vulnerable.

Harry seemed to realize how open Red was at that moment and bent down to kiss him as he gently jacked Red's leaking cock. Red hissed, knowing how close to the edge he was. Harry gave a soft chuckle and leaned over Red to get the lube, the soft hair on his chest tickling Red's nose.

He took his time to prepare Red, refusing to hurry, letting Red work through the burn until he could breathe again. He teased Red's sweet spot with his fingers until Red was begging and crying for his cock. He could have been embarrassed at how loud and needy he was, but Harry encouraged it, telling him he wanted to hear more.

Then Harry locked gazes with him and nothing else mattered to Red except the love in Harry's eyes as he filled Red to the root and began to move.

Red closed his eyes as he drew closer to his orgasm. He felt it curl low in his belly, his balls drawing up tight, his whole focus narrowed down to the thick cock driving him higher, harder, tighter. He exploded with a yell, spurting over his belly and chest. At the same time hearing Harry roaring his climax above him as he pushed into Red so hard, they moved several inches up the bed and Red had to push away the pillows that threatened to fall on him.

A few more shaky thrusts and Harry collapsed with a *whoosh* onto him, breathing heavily in his ear.

"Fuck, boy, what you do to me," Harry panted before he managed to roll them onto their sides, facing each other, so they were away from the wet patch. Their legs entangled, and his hands smoothed down Red's skin as if he were learning a lost language.

Red sucked in deep breaths as his breathing slowed. He was covered in sweat and cum, but he didn't care. He just wanted to stay close to Harry.

"Are you all right, my boy?" Harry asked. "Not too sore?"

He blushed and pressed his face into the pillow, not able to meet Harry's gaze at that moment.

"Boy?"

Red knew he wasn't going to get away with not answering. "I'm a little sore but it's fine. Thank you for caring for me."

Harry reached forward and pressed a kiss on his lips. "I'll always take care of you."

"I never thought it could be like this," Red admitted, awed. He knew this feeling would stay with him forever. He'd found love even when he wasn't looking for it.

They kissed again, learning about each other in the darkness, until a thought occurred to Red.

"I have no idea how to be a boy," he admitted.

"It's the way it's meant to be," Harry assured him. "I have so much to teach you, Red."

"And I have so much to give you, my Daddy."

And that was something Red never thought he'd be able to offer. Himself, to a man who loved him.

The night moved on as they lay together, stripes of moonlight across their entwined bodies, heated breaths joining into one as the Daddy and his boy explored each other with infinite tenderness.

———

One year later

"You know he's gonna hate me for this," Red muttered to Jack who just shrugged as he tied on the hat and dress.

"He'll growl and bitch, then you'll apologize, flutter your eyelashes and he'll pin you down and fuck you."

"Is that what you do with PJ?"

Jack smirked. "My Daddy is easily tamed."

Red decided that was Jack's way of saying PJ was a man of simple pleasures. But he probably had a point. He climbed into the freshly made bed and stared at Jack.

"Okay, bring it on."

Jack regarded him for a moment. "There's something really creepy about seeing you dressed like that."

"Said the man who put elephant poop on the wall," Red shot back.

Jack flipped him off, then laughed. "You have a point."

"Just get him here before I lose my nerve."

Red was two seconds away from declaring this was stupid, even though it had been his idea in the first place.

Jack bounced over to the bed and hugged him. "Take a deep breath, brother mine. You're doing this to please your Daddy."

Hugging him back, Red realized two things for certain. One, he had a family for the first time. The boys had declared they were brothers too. And Jack was right. Red wanted to please his Daddy.

HARRY

Harry finished mucking out Thunder's stall, wondering where his errant boy was. Red had promised him he would come help him with the horses after his lesson with Gruff.

The school lessons for the Kingdom boys were still ongoing and although Red didn't need them now, he was there to support Gruff as the number of boys needing their help increased. There was talk of building a school and Red had investigated training to become a teacher.

"If my boy doesn't turn up soon, I'm gonna hunt him down, put him over my knee, and tan his sweet butt until it's as red as his hair," Harry informed Star who was in the next stall.

She ignored him and carried on lipping at her hay. Harry sighed. None of the horses paid the slightest attention if he ranted, especially if it was about what he'd do to Red. It was as if they all knew he would only do what Red wanted and they'd both enjoy it. Red loved having his ass spanked as much as Harry enjoyed doing it.

By the time he'd finished, there was still no sign of Red and Harry stomped back to the cabin, ready to spank his boy good.

The conversation around the table died as Harry opened the kitchen door.

"Why're you staring at me like that?" he grumbled. "Where's Red?"

"Uh, why aren't you—" Jake stopped as Aaron slapped a hand over his mouth.

Brad loped over to Harry's side. "Ok, little bro, you should be somewhere else right now. Like hours ago. Didn't you get Jack's message?"

Harry blinked at him. "What message? Where?"

"Your phone, idiot."

Brad held out his hand and Harry handed him his phone. "It's turned off."

"He's gonna kill you," Vinny muttered.

"What the hell are you talking about?" Harry demanded.

Brad sighed and looked at his brothers. "Okay, Brenners. Here's what we're going to do. Lyle, you message Red. Aaron, get the cape. It's on his bed. Damien, give me your scarf. Quit grumbling, it's the right color. Me and PJ will take him there. Jack, where's the basket?"

Confused, Harry stood as his brothers and their boys disappeared, only to return a minute later. Brad had hold of his bicep as if he thought Harry was going to bolt. It was on Harry's mind.

"Where's my boy?" he asked Brad, who ignored him.

Damien handed over a red scarf to Brad. "You'd better not lose this. It was Dad's."

"He won't. Shut up." Brad tied the scarf around Harry's eyes. Harry went to rip it off, but Brad snapped, "Don't make me cuff you."

"He'd enjoy that far too much," PJ crowed.

Harry went as red as his hair. How the hell did PJ know that? The cackle from PJ ended with a hiss from Jack. Harry sighed. Red had told Jack, who'd told PJ.

Then he felt something being draped around his shoulders. He touched it and the material was soft and velvety, like something a kid would wear to play dress-up, although it was huge, falling around his ankles.

"It's gonna smell of horses," Vinny said, but Damien hushed him.

"Basket," Brad ordered. "PJ, get the quad bike. It's too dark to send him walking."

"On it," PJ said.

Every time Harry opened his mouth, Brad told him to keep quiet. He gave up in the end and waited for them to finish with their tomfoolery.

"I can't get hold of him," Lyle sounded worried.

"We'll call you if there's a problem," Brad said.

"Get hold of who? Red?" Now Harry was the worried one.

But Brad just manhandled Harry out of the kitchen door and guided him onto the quad. "Here's the basket. Hang onto it. I'll be next to you."

They bumped up the unmade road. Harry was no fool. Cape and basket, it was kind of obvious what was going on. The question was, why?

The quad stopped. Harry was relieved. Not being able to see was disconcerting and his stomach gave an uneasy lurch. Brad helped him off, then smacked his arm. "Enjoy, Little Red Riding Daddy!"

Then he and PJ were gone, leaving Harry standing on the path alone. He ripped off the scarf and looked around. He was outside one of the new cabins the brothers were slowly building for their homes. This one was almost complete, with a wood stove and electricity.

Harry walked in to find the place warm, although the wood stove needed attention. He peeked in the basket. Dinner. And lube! His brothers knew him well. Harry's stomach rumbled but he placed the basket on the kitchen counter, added more wood to the stove, and went in search of his boy, lube in hand. He found him in the bedroom.

Red was curled up in the bed fast asleep. He was dressed in an old lady nightie and a wolf mask that had slipped off his face. It was kind of creepy. He may have been wearing a hat, but that was on the floor now.

Harry bent down and pressed a kiss to Red's mouth. "Wake up, Granny. Little Red Riding Daddy is here to feed you."

Red moaned and brushed his mouth. "You didn't come."

Oh, Harry had every intention of coming...and coming.

"I'm late, but I'm here now."

Red's copper eyelashes fluttered open to show his beautiful blue eyes. "Daddy...I mean Little Red Riding Daddy. I waited for you, but you didn't show."

"I'm sorry," Harry said sincerely. "My phone had died. But why are you here?"

"I thought you'd like to christen our new home."

Harry stared at him. "What?"

Red's smile was brilliant. "This is our home. Your brothers decided we could have this one."

Harry swallowed hard around the lump in his throat. This cabin had been planned for Damien and Vinny. His family was just the best and he would make sure they all knew it.

"You knew about this?" Harry demanded.

"I did. We wanted to give you a present. It's from all of us for keeping your dreams here."

After months of vacillation, Harry had finally admitted that he didn't want to go out of state to college. He didn't want to go to school away from home. He wanted to stay on the mountain with his boy and his family. Damien had sobbed on his shoulder like the sappy bear he was when Harry told them his change of plans over dinner one night. Maybe Harry shed a few tears too when they all hugged him fiercely. Red just looked resigned.

His boy had tried hard to fit in, and he'd grown to love being part of the family, but he'd wanted a home of his own. Once Harry had decided not to move away, Red struggled with the lack of privacy. Now they could have their own space and the family close by.

"I'm going to show you just how happy you make me, Granny Red." Harry rolled Red beneath him, pushing him down into the bed.

"Why, Little Red Riding Daddy, what big...arms you have," Red said, somewhat breathlessly.

Harry grinned at the obvious hesitation. "All the better to hug you with, my boy." Maybe they'd swapped roles, but he didn't care.

Then Harry kissed Red on the mouth, devouring him until his boy was boneless in his arms.

"What a mouth you have," Red murmured.

Harry gave him a wicked smile. "All the better to suck you down the back of my throat and make you howl, my boy."

He pressed down into Red who sighed lustily.

"What a big cock you have, Little Red Riding Daddy."

"I do. Just so you can ride me hard."

From Red's wolfish grin in return, he approved of the adult version of this fairy tale. "Can we quit playing games and just get naked, Daddy?"

"First one naked gets a blowjob," Harry suggested, and grinned as Red skinned out of his clothes with abandon.

He took it slower. After all, the first thing he was going to do was make his boy howl. That was the way all fairy tales should end in this Daddy's opinion.

The End

From Sue Brown:

Thank you for joining me in the Bearytales world again. It's been a while, but I'm so happy to be back with the Brenners and their boys again. Snow Twink now heads the family and Brad's story will finish it off. But in the meantime, it's time Alec and Matt resolved their on/off, rinse-repeat relationship in ***Beauty & the Boy***.

———

This was the bonus scene for Snow Twink. I've put it here for you to get a little flavor of Alec and Matt. They were always meant to be #3 in the series, but Jake and Aaron shouted louder.

This story is a teaser for the forthcoming series. You didn't think I was going to leave it there, did you? There are some old friends and new in this taster for Alec's story. Josh Cooper is **from Angel Securities** *and Quinn Ryder is from* **Biker Daddy Bodyguards**.

Alec watched Damien and Gruff arguing with Jake. They were in the small barn away from the house. It was bitterly cold, and they were dressed in hats, jackets, and gloves as they paced around the small space. Alec let Jake do the talking. He was more interested in watching what was going on.

For example, he wondered if Damien knew Vinny was hiding in a corner of the barn, his gaze fixed on Damien as he paced around. The boy didn't look at anyone else.

Lyle sat on a bale of hay watching the discussion. Well, watching Griff, but mainly listening. He hadn't tried to join in, but from the deep frown, he clearly wasn't happy with the discussion.

Damien turned on his heel and said for the tenth time, "No. You're not going to Kingdom Island. Gruff and Lyle are right. You'll never get out alive."

Jake threw his hands up. "We're not kids, Damien. We know what we're doing."

"No, you don't. This isn't some kids' game. Now we know there are more orphanages we can leave it to the authorities to handle it. I don't want you getting involved."

Alec let them get on with it. Jake had agreed to take the family fire while Alec did the digging. They would ignore him while Jake was shouting. It was how the two of them usually worked. It was amazing how much they'd achieved over the years and no one in their family had noticed.

Of course, Damien and PJ were tied up with the farm,

Harry only cared about the horses, and Brad wanted to blow things up and then write poetry about it. Alec wasn't sure what Gruff had done before Lyle arrived. The youngest Brenner had tended to stay out of everyone's way. Now he was teaching Lyle and Vinny to read and write. He was really good at it too. There was talk of more of the boys coming to the cabin so that Gruff could tutor them.

Which left Alec and Jake running a successful investigations business on the downlow. The worse Jake could make them look, the better.

"Look, we should leave this to the cops," Damien barked.

Jake raised an eyebrow. "The cops. Like the sheriff who was in David Rogerson's pocket? Yeah, those cops?"

Damien let out an explosive breath. "I don't want anything to happen to you."

He was clearly shaken up by Gruff being poisoned and Lyle being kidnapped. They all were, Alec included. Things like this didn't happen to their family. They laughed and joked about being seven gay daddies under one roof, but they lived normal lives, managing a Christmas tree farm. Even the investigations business was focused on what happened to other people, not them. But the minute Gruff had come home with a half-frozen boy with an incredible tale, their lives had changed.

If they thought rescuing a hundred orphaned boys was hard enough, nothing prepared them for discovering more Kingdoms, and each one had its evil CEO. Alec's heart ached for the boys trapped within their walls, and he wasn't prepared to let them stay there for a minute longer than he had to.

But first, he needed information. And maybe he was intrigued too. He'd never been to the Kingdom Mountain theme park. It had always been out of their reach as children, and as an adult, he'd been too busy to take the time out to spend a day there. Now that was closed and the nearest one was Kingdom Island.

Jake was shouting again. Alec forced himself to listen.

"How many boys are you willing to sacrifice, Damien? One? Ten? A hundred?"

"Don't be so melodramatic," Damien muttered, but Alec could see he was starting to weaken. His eldest brother had the softest heart of any of them under the surly exterior. He just needed a little more pushing.

Alec looked over at Vinny. His gaze was still fixed on Damien.

"If Gruff hadn't found me, I would be another statistic," Lyle said.

Gruff was by his side in an instant, his arms around Lyle, holding him so tenderly Alec was sure Gruff had forgotten about everyone else in the barn. Only Lyle mattered. Deep down, Alec had to admit he was envious of their relationship.

Jake sighed. "I don't know about anyone else, but it makes me sick to my stomach to think of these boys being whored out to the management or 'disappearing'."

Alec knew what the air quotes meant. They all did.

Jake continued. "How many bodies of young men have we found over the years? How many of them were cast-offs from Kingdom Mountain? We thought they were hikers."

Damien slumped against a post. Jake cast a glance at Alec who gave the briefest of nods. Leave it there. No need to overplay their hand.

"I'm freezing," Alec grumbled. "Let's go back to the house."

Damien stomped out of the barn and Vinny joined him

immediately, his hand going in Damien's. From his eldest brother's lack of surprise, Alec surmised Damien had known he was there all along.

Gruff glanced between Alec and Jake. "I hope you know what you're doing." He laughed at their wide-eyed stares. "I may be your youngest brother but I'm not stupid. Damien may be oblivious but I'm not. I know the games you two play. Just keep your heads down, okay? You know how high the costs are." He tugged Lyle to his feet, and they followed Damien and Vinny out of the barn.

"Gruff never fails to surprise me," Alec muttered. Then he grinned at Jake. "Game on?"

"Game on," Jake agreed with a smirk.

They waited a while before leaving the barn, talking over details of their planned excursion to Kingdom Island theme park.

Jake grimaced. "Damien's right about one thing. This is above our pay grade. It might be time to call in Angel Enterprises."

"Good idea. I'll call them when we get back," Alec said.

"I'll call them. You ought to call Matt. See if he's free to come as the bratty younger brother."

Alec pulled a face at the thought of calling one of their freelancers. "Do I have to? You know what he's like. He's gonna spend the whole time trying to get into my pants."

Jake snorted out a laugh. "If you just put him over your knee and spanked his ass once in a while, he'd leave you alone."

Alec grunted. He'd thought the same himself, but he was concerned the young man wanted more than an occasional spanking. He'd seen the longing looks Matt threw his way and then the boy had run away. Matt didn't know what he wanted, and Alec wasn't going to force him to stay.

But Jake was right. Having Matt along would disguise the group even more.

When he was back in his bedroom, Alec pulled out his phone and scrolled down to Matt's number.

"Well, hello, Alec. Have you finally decided to make me all yours, Daddy Bear?" Matt's liquid voice purred in his ear.

Alec rolled his eyes. The boy was never going to change. Flirt and run. Flirt and run. "In your dreams, Matt. I have a job for you."

"About time," Matt said, "I was beginning to think you didn't love me anymore."

"It's harvest time," Alec said shortly. "Busy. But this case has come up."

"What do you need?"

"Bratty younger brother."

"I can do that. We could always play step-brothers." That wicked purr was back again.

"Moving on."

Matt laughed at Alec's deflection. "So where are we going?"

"I need you to come to a meeting."

"It's serious then."

Alec could hear the surprise in Matt's voice. "It's serious, boy."

"Daddy Bear, I'm all yours."

Alec disconnected the call and stared up at the ceiling. "If only you were, my boy. If only you were."

———

Alec and Jake were small-town operatives. When they discovered the evil extended beyond Kingdom Mountain theme park, they knew they needed outside help. Josh Cooper from Angel Securities seemed the right person to approach. What Angel Securities did was somewhat nebulous, but in the chatter in their world, if you needed a job that was outside your scope, they were the ones to approach.

Alec recognized him the second he walked in. With his slight figure in a designer suit and long black wool coat, he looked out of place in the town café.

"He looks like a kid playing dress-up," Jake muttered.

But Alec knew from his reputation never to underestimate Josh Cooper. It had a way of biting you on the ass.

What they didn't expect was his companion. Alec clocked him as a Daddy the second he strode into the café in black leathers. He glanced at Jake who nodded in agreement.

"Now why did Cooper bring him?"

"Let's find out."

Alec got to his feet and waved. The Daddy saw them, caught Cooper's arm, and they headed in their direction.

Cooper spoke as soon as he reached them. "Tell me you have good coffee here. Brits can't do coffee." His accent was pure Manhattan.

Behind him, the Daddy rolled his eyes. "You chain-drank coffee all the way here."

His accent was harder to place. Maybe Oregon? Alec needed to work on that.

Jake laughed. "They told me you'd say that. Tell me what you need."

He took their order and vanished toward the baristas and Alec held out his hand.

"Alec Brenner."

Cooper's handshake was firmer than he expected. "Josh

Cooper and this is Quinn Ryder. I thought his skills would be useful."

Neither of them said what his skills were as Ryder shook his hand. He was about the size of Alec but whereas Alec was a bear, Ryder was something else. Alec found it hard to put his finger on it. Muscle. Dangerous.

"Your proposal was interesting," Cooper said as he took off his coat and laid it over the back of a chair.

So they were starting business straight away. He could appreciate that.

"Let's wait for Jake to come back," he murmured. Matt was late as usual, but Alec could fill him in later.

Cooper inclined his head and sat down. Ryder sat next to him and Alec noticed he didn't stop looking around the whole time.

Bodyguard, maybe?

Reputation said Cooper didn't need a bodyguard.

Jake returned and after Cooper had taken a long slug of coffee with a happy sigh, he put his cup down and stared at them.

"Why are we here?"

"We have a job and it's bigger than us." Jake took the front seat, his tone blunt as usual.

Cooper nodded. "So I see. But what makes you think we can help?"

"You saw the proposal," Alec said. "We're talking a national disaster. Boys vanishing behind fairy tale walls for years and then being killed. We're small-town private investigators. We don't have the skills to take on these people."

"You could leave it with Angel Enterprises," Ryder suggested. "This is bread and butter to them."

To Alec's surprise, Cooper shot Ryder an irritated look. "We're spooks, not kid-hunters."

"If you say so," Ryder murmured.

"We're desperate." Jake interrupted Cooper and Ryder's glare-off.

Cooper huffed, tapped his fingers on the table, huffed again, and finally nodded. "You're right. This has to be stopped." He glanced at Ryder who nodded in agreement.

Alec felt the tension drain out of Jake. Cooper admitting their instincts were right was huge.

Jake nudged him. "Matt's here."

Alec stood and waved as Matt came into the café. The boy's cheeks and nose were pinked from the cold. He looked adorable in a plaid jacket and skinny jeans. Alec smiled as he realized Matt wore the hat Alec had given him.

"Cute," Cooper murmured. "Pretty."

Alec glared at him and Ryder rolled his eyes.

"Just ignore him, Brenner. He flirts with every man with a pulse, but he's not allowed to touch. His husband would kill you."

You, not him. Interesting.

Cooper pouted and Alec laughed, relaxing now he knew no one was making a play for his boy. And yes, Matt was his boy even if he didn't know it yet.

"Daddy Bear," Matt cooed as he bounced over to him and kissed him on the cheek.

Alec growled. And blushed. And growled a bit more. That boy was going to be put over his knee if he wasn't careful.

He was fully aware of Cooper's highly amused smirk.

"Hey, Jake." Matt leaned over and kissed him too. "And who are these gorgeous..." He trailed off as he studied Quinn Ryder.

Alec had never seen Matt speechless before. He didn't like it. Ryder oozed Daddy and dominance, and Matt responded to it.

Ryder held out his hand to Matt. "Quinn Ryder."

Matt took his hand and said somewhat breathlessly, "Matt George."

Alec wanted to yank Matt's hand out of Ryder's. Matt was his.

Get yourself under control, Brenner.

Matt was a free agent. If he wanted to play breathy boy with a Daddy well above Alec in the food chain, there was nothing Alec could do about it.

"Down boy, he's taken too," Cooper said, rolling his eyes at Alec.

"Okay, now we're all here. Let's get down to business," Jake said, still smirking at Alec. "Cooper, Ryder, we want to scout the nearest of the theme parks, but to be fair, Josh and I don't know what we're looking for. That's where Angel Securities comes in."

Matt furrowed his brow. "Where did you say we were going?"

"We're going out for the day to investigate," Alec said. "Kingdom Island theme park."

Silence.

Matt stared at him, so pale Alec thought he was about to pass out.

"Matt, are you all right, boy?"

"I can't." Matt sounded so shaky. "I can't, Daddy Bear, I can't."

Alec wrapped an arm around him and held him close, feeling the boy's heart thumping close to his own. "You can't what, my boy?"

"Come with you to the Island theme park. I can't do it. I swore I'd never go back there."

"Why not, Matt?" Cooper asked, all flirtatiousness vanished as he got down to business.

Matt tilted his head to look at Alec, rather than Cooper. "Because they'll kill me."

Read **Beauty & the Boy**, *a second chance, Beauty and the Beast romance in the **Bearytales in the Wood** world.*

In a world of second chances, will Matt get the one he needs most?

Alec has been patient, but he's waited long enough. It's time for his boy to make up his mind, stay or go. Why won't he commit to their happy ever after?

All Alec wants is an answer from Matt, a confirmation that he wants to spend the rest of his life in his Daddy's arms. But Matt refuses to commit. Instead, he seems to be pulling away.

Matt knows his Daddy Bear wants a life together, but he is still not sure he can give that to him. Matt knows he's broken inside, the beast in their relationship. Something must be wrong for him not to be able to say yes to his beautiful and loving Daddy.

Then Matt's hidden secret, his monster, is exposed and threatens to destroy his relationship with Alec and the Brenners once and for all. Will Alec support his boy as their world crumbles around them? Will Matt run away rather than ask for what he needs?

In the sixth book of Bearytales, will this Daddy and boy get their happy ever after?

Thank you for reading ***Boy Riding***.
If you have time to leave a review at Amazon I'd be very grateful.

Come and get all of Sue's latest news by signing up for her newsletter here.

ALSO BY SUE BROWN

You can find all of Sue's books over at Amazon. Don't forget to sign up for her newsletter here.

ABOUT SUE BROWN

Cranky middle-aged author with an addiction to coffee, and a passion for romancing two guys. She loves her dog, she loves her kids, and she loves coffee; which order very much depends on the time of day.

Come over and talk to Sue at:

Newsletter: http://bit.ly/SueBrownNews
Bookbub: https://www.bookbub.com/profile/sue-brown
TikTok: https://www.tiktok.com/@suebrownstories
Patreon: https://www.patreon.com/suebrownstories
Her website: http://www.suebrownstories.com/
Author group – Facebook: https://www.facebook.com/groups/suebrownstories/
Facebook: https://www.facebook.com/SueBrownsStories/
Email: sue@suebrownstories.com

Printed in Great Britain
by Amazon